MEMOIRS OF A GONE WORLD

MARTIN BAX is a consultant paediatrician who has now retired from clinical work and is an honorary reader in Child Health at Imperial College, London. In addition to his medical career he founded the arts magazine *Ambit* in 1959, which continues to this day. *Ambit* has published poetry, prose and artwork from people such as Fleur Adcock, Peter Porter, Tenessee Williams, JG Ballard, Peter Blake, Eduoardo Paolozzi, Carol Ann Duffy and many others. He has written two novels: *The Hospital Ship*, published by Picador and New Directions in 1978, and *Love on the Borders* published by Seren in 2005. In the 1970s, using text from *The Hospital Ship*, he developed the *Vietnam Symphony* with jazz trumpeter Henry Lowther, which was performed at the Institute of Contemporary Arts and broadcast on BBC Radio 3. He has also written for children and his book *Edmund Went Far Away*, illustrated by Michael Foreman, was published in the UK and USA.

MARTIN BAX

MEMOIRS OF A GONE WORLD

SALT

LONDON

PUBLISHED BY SALT PUBLISHING

Fourth Floor, 2 Tavistock Place, Bloomsbury, London WC1H 9RA United Kingdom

First published 2010

Printed in Great Britain by the MPG Books Group, Bodmin and King's Lynn

Typeset in Swift 11 / 14

ISBN 978 1 84471 476 6 paperback

1 3 5 7 9 8 6 4 2

CONTENTS

THE TURNED-IN, BROKEN-UP AND GONE WORLD

(For Robert Sward and Ann Quin)

IT WAS CAROLINE WHO sounded the first note of alarm. She was copulating with a man when his penis broke off at the root. The affair had been a casual one. She had gone off to inspect the very latest bit of the scene, a vast hall with coloured slides in vivid greens and purples shot at the walls and incessant thump of electronic music. The company was mostly young, variously dressed and appeared partially bemused. Caroline wandered round for a while and then, being an immensely practical girl, decided there was nothing in it for her with the possible exception of some rather bizarre sex. You could say she got that. She recalled that she had never been taken by a man with those long droopy moustaches, so she drifted up to a suitable specimen and began to make his acquaintance.

Caroline thought him rather slow at understanding her. But then, as I have pointed out to her, there are not many who have her quality of directness. This, mixed with the rather surprised expression she always wears on her face, often confuses the object of her intentions and makes him wonder whether it's her or him who's being naive. However, that's an aside. One gathers that, in time, the man began to make some suitable response and, in time, they found themselves uncomfortably ensconced on the rather hard floor in the dim candlelight at the extreme edge of the building.

When the unique event occurred, Caroline was half into an orgasm and, for a moment, even she was unable to react. The 'man' reared back and in the dim light Caroline had a glimpse of an epicene and hairless crotch before the man pulled up his jeans.

'Sorry, love,' he said, 'I broke up a bit,' and he drifted off into the haze. Caroline removed what was left of the organ from her body, dropping it distastefully to the ground where, to her amazement, it rapidly crumbled to dust. Hastily adjusting her own clothes and, fearing for the permanence of her own anatomy, Caroline left the building.

Later that night she called me up to report the incident. 'The worst thing,' she said, 'was that he didn't seem to mind. It was almost as if he'd been waiting for it to happen.'

In the morning I was inclined to wonder if I'd not dreamt the whole conversation and debated calling back to check her story. But it was the usual working day, so I settled to my desk. I was flipping through my standard mass of abstracts when I was held up for a while by a *Science* reprint (Cohen *et al.*, 1967). Someone had fed it me, I suppose, to get my reaction. It reported a twofold increase in chromosome breaks in leucocytes treated with lysergic acid diethylamide in vitro.

The breaks had occurred even at a dosage as low as $0.001ug/ml$ and after exposures of only four hours. The experimenters had followed up by looking for patients on the drugs and, sure enough, found a rate of 200 cells in metaphase with the breaks. This represented a rate of 12.7%, as opposed to the normal 3.7%. There was some doubt about whether this actual drug was responsible for the damage in the patients and the authors, with proper caution, pointed out that they had other features which distinguished them from the control group. The drug might merely have been an activator triggering off a mechanism already latent within the organism.

It was this impression of the suggestibility of the organism—the human organism—which worried me. There was other evidence of this suggestibility all around me. There was a call to be aware of the inner man, of the essential nature of human life (whatever that meant). A need seemed to have sprung up for meditation, for a going apart; people spoke vaguely of the East. They mentioned only the atmosphere of events, said nothing of what they were actually about. Leading poets were heard protesting that these were the new necessities. The lost penis, the meditant world, the broken chromosome, all seemed to me to be signs of some impending disaster. The human race was heading for something which it could, if it wished, resist but it had lost the will to do that.

Naturally, I followed up the drug lead a bit. But it was a blind alley. There were a few more relevant articles and a good bit of pontificating in the British Medical Journal (1967), as usual. There seemed to be some sort of campaign in favour of a relatively innocuous euphoriant, but there wasn't much to that. I contented myself by rereading Joyce's words (1966) which concluded with his famous phrase: 'society gets the poisons it asks for.' Caroline had gone out of town for the weekend but was back on Monday. She rang me to report on a British hill fort she had visited and of two badgers she'd seen in the moonlight. Those animals never come out for me.

For ten days nothing further developed and my anxieties

had somewhat dissipated, but then came the outbreak of the 'Gone Disease'. I was walking through the Casualty department and observed the most bizarre-looking patient being wheeled in from an ambulance. The crew handled him with some distaste, but two policeman who were with them had shed some of their normal solidity and appeared genuinely worried. They shouted loudly for the doctor and then rushed back to help lift the patient off the trolly, although this was unnecessary as the weight when recorded later proved to be well under 5 stone. The police reported that the patient had been found propped up against a wall on an open garage site not far from the hospital, but they knew nothing else.

As it happened, the whole medical intake team was in Casualty and I joined them, so there was no shortage of interested observers. There were no legs beyond the mid-thigh, but we were surprised that we could find no sign of any amputation scars. The same went for the arms, although parts of the forearms were still present and the elbow joints were intact. The arms ended in a rounded point about two inches above the wrist. The face was pale but not sweating, the cheeks were somewhat indrawn, the eyes not fully closed nor fully open, and the eyeballs mostly rolled up, but occasionally they flashed down so that the pupils could be seen. There was no response to questioning and quite sharp painful stimuli failed to elicit a cry.

The posture was remarkable. The patient would not lie down and, when not held down, bobbed up into an erect position. The arms were held crossed in front of the chest and it was difficult to prise them apart. The whole attitude reminded me forcibly of the film I had once seen of the anencephalic baby which Gamper made and on which Bates (1967) had recently provided some notes. The extraordinary finding was that at three months the motor behaviour was actually in advance of a normal child's but its stereotyped and automatic features were evidence of the absence of the 'new' brain which reorganises subhuman activity into the sophisticated repertoire of activity which distinguishes man from other mammalian species.

An eager medical student started at once to try and look at the retinae through his opthalmoscope. He suddenly let out a cry: 'There are colours inside his head!' The medical registrar grabbed the instrument and himself peered into the eyes. Then he dropped it, looked at me—the most senior man present—and said in a worried voice, 'He's right.'

I took up the opthalmoscope—a standard Keeler model—and focused on the spot where I thought the pupil would next appear when the eyeballs rolled down. To my amazement I suddenly had a glimpse, not of the fundi and retinal vessels slowly pulsating, but of a vivid vibrating green light which almost dazzled me. Then the eye rolled up, but I waited for it to come down again and this time I was assaulted by a luminous orange. Something funny was happening right inside the head.

The clothes were mere rags and as we tried to take them off they fragmented in our hands. As I feared, there were no genitals, female or male, visible and I was startled to notice that even the nipples had gone. The anus was present and perforate, but around that orifice and elsewhere the body was hairless, except for a little stubble on the head. I had to go to my own clinic so I said to the registrar, 'I should get your boss down at once. And I suggest among your other investigations you do the nuclear sex.' I don't really know why that seemed important, but at the same time I felt one must find out the gender of our patient.

My clinic was a small one. Although I didn't know it, the birth rate was already dropping. The mothers were quiet and the children unusually subdued. The students sat silent and looked bored. I can't have been a very stimulating teacher that afternoon. Shortly before 4 p.m., I dismissed them and, refusing my normal cup of tea, went into the wards in search of the patient. I was not surprised to find that he or she had eventually been admitted to a neurological ward—no one else would accept the case.

I learnt that there had been a disturbing scene as the stretcher had reached the ward. The patient was still sitting upright, his arms folded and looking like some evil reincarnation of a desiccated buddha. In the ward there was a terminal cancer patient with several secondaries in his brain. He had not spoken for several days, he was heavily sedated and thought to be unaware of what was going on around him. He had shot up in bed as the little procession entered the ward and cried out in a high-pitched voice, 'It's the Man from the Gone World!'

This, together with the bizarre appearance of the new patient, had disturbed the other patients on the ward considerably, but Sister had managed to settle them down again around the television set by the time I arrived.

Not surprisingly, Sister had consequently decided to put the patient in a side ward and it was there I found him with Ian, our brilliant young neurologist, peering at some X-rays.

'Hallo, David,' he said. 'Your idea to have him nuclear sexed, I hear. Well it is a him, or rather, none of the cells have any Barr bodies, so they're assuming he's male, but the nuclei are all breaking up. The cytogenetics boys are all running round in circles with excitement. Look at these bones, though. It's really weird, they look almost as if they're melting away.'

'What are you going to do?'

'Stuff him full of anabolic steroids for tonight and biopsy his brain in the morning to see if I can explain those lights inside—not that I think I will.' What Ian did not realise was that by morning his patient would be gone.

Ian had suggested we keep quiet about this terrifying case, but some of his colleagues were less cautious and the evening papers were full of it. In any event there was a rush of cases the next day and by the following week the hospitals were swamped. The government was pressed into urgent action, unnerved as they were by the loss of the Prime Minister, who was one of the first to go. They set up seven clinical centres with attached research groups, but also realising the catastrophic nature of the process, asked several people to form independent groups attacking the problem from any angle they saw fit. I was asked to head up one of these basic research groups and for some weeks worked night and day looking for some answer to the Gone Disease.

This focusing on the biological aspects of our disaster alone was, I now believe, unfortunate, but for the record I will just briefly conclude the chronicle of my personal involvement in the situation and indicate the line I followed in the immediate weeks. The clinical groups quickly established that what was happening was a rapid and radical break-up of the protein molecules. The basic carbon linkages no longer held together and within a few days the patients just disintegrated into water vapour, gases and not much else. A little phosphate ash was all one found in the beds of the Gone patients. Of course, the clinicians looked for some infective cause for this break-up and tried desperately to find an agent which would reverse, stop or delay the disintegration. Steroids, as Ian had thought, were the obvious line, but it took some time to prove they were useless as so many patients were gone before treatment could be properly initiated.

My own feeling was that we were up against something that was undermining the very roots of life itself. I started therefore with the work reported by Mathews and Moser from St Louis (1967). They bombarded a mixture of methane gas and ammonia with electricity; their product formed a black compound which, in the presence of water, turned to a brown scum. They believed that life itself had originally evolved from this scum. I decided to see how the 'scum' was behaving under the new conditions and to see if I could introduce anything into the reaction which would speed up the rate of formation; from there I hoped . . . Well, anyway, I got as far as demonstrating that the stuff was taking twice as long to form as it ought to and was breaking down spontaneously, which it ought not to. By the time we discovered that, the break-up had become widespread.

Car accidents had begun to increase. At first one thought it was fear of the Gone Disease. Then suddenly there was a series of disasters on the American local airlines, a wing fell off a Comet while it was taxiing at London airport and the suburban rail service collapsed as the rails themselves twisted, shrunk and broke into pieces. I began to realise that my own approach had been foolish and unimaginative; we were not dealing with a disease process—the whole human world was breaking up. When one of my assistant's hands broke off as he was handing me a preparation, I realised the futility of going on with my work at the institute. We were all members of a going, going, gone world.

In the next few days, the pace of the break-up accelerated. Cars ceased to function altogether. A tyre would go flat and as you changed that one, the other three would slowly subside. The steering wheels fell away, the dashboard became a blank and the whole car shrank into itself. The lights refused to shine out but illuminated the useless engines. Outward appearances were sometimes deceptive; things looked all right, but when one looked into them closely, one found that things were sadly astray. One took down books only to find that words no longer existed, the letters had all elided and if the process had gone further, whole pages would be completely blank. As with people, there was a selectivity: the romantic novelists naturally went first, and then many of the poets. Sometimes one opened a book only to find that the pages had faded away and only the covers remained. The Russian novelists did quite well, but most history books just collapsed. I was pleased to find in one library I visited a complete *Gibbon* surviving after everything else had gone; but even there, poor old Dean Milman's notes had just slid off the pages.

They tried hard to keep the wireless going as long as possible, but gave it up when the very waves in the air seemed to fragment. Music no longer made any sense when a single note from a single instrument reached you by itself and moments later a whole rush of sound would reach one all at once in a frantic rush of harmonics and sub-harmonics. Radio announcers' voices just broke.

Houses shut down too. Curtains would not stay pulled back and where there were blinds, they just ran down. Slowly, the whole building would begin to shrink: the windows disappearing, shutting up like eyes in a totally smooth face and leaving no trace of where they had been. One would hear of a house that had stayed open and rush over there to see if one could get in. Often as not, one could not find the door and if one could, it would not open. People who were still there stopped going out. Anyway, the roads and sidewalks were breaking up. All the dogs and cats had died.

It was difficult to know how to proceed. Hospital work was meaningless. There were no new babies for me to examine. Pregnant women failed to deliver, their wombs reabsorbed the foetuses, their pelvises shrank, their breasts involuted. Children were certainly dying from lack of care, but they were not being brought to the hospitals that remained, they were shrinking away, crushed among the crumbling houses. I tried to go around in my own area and help a little, but it was no use; people shrank from contact. They wanted to spend their last days alone with their own selves.

Finally, I just stayed in my flat. It seemed to be bearing up rather well. All the lights had gone, of course; the light bulbs disappearing up the wires from which they hung and the electricity was off. Curiously, water still flowed in the taps and I decided I should try and wait it out there where I was. During the day I could read and most of my books, I found, were still surviving. I got a car battery and fixed up my gramophone to run off it. Many of the records were still there, although I found several empty cases. Other records seemed perfectly all right, but when I put them on no sound came out. *My Fair Lady* was a case in point. As depression deepened, I tended to spend more and more time in bed.

It was there that Caroline found me. I was lying dreaming of fragmenting carbon chains, the bonds snapping derisively at me, when suddenly the images fled. Someone was shaking me awake.

'Come on, David, come on.' I struggled up and looked at her. She was quite unchanged.

She laughed at the intense stare I gave her.

'You're not gone, then,' I said.

'What, me?' she said and laughed again. 'Did you think they'd get me? I was a bit worried about you. Come on, we're off.'

I do not intend to chronicle the succeeding days. Indeed, were I to do so, you might not remain convinced of my veracity. I will merely state that some long time later, I found myself with three other men and Caroline living a sort of South Sea Island life on a beach in southern Turkey. There were the remnants of some holiday camp and we each settled into a cabin of our own. This saved us the bother of building, but otherwise, in a leisurely sort of way, it was the true primitive stuff. How we got there is irrelevant, as is most of what we did. We cooked, we fished, we swept inland in search of animals or men—found none, except for a mate for the cock we had with us. That was encouraging. Spent the days mainly alone swimming, wondering why we bothered. All too full of memories for talk or action.

One night I was lying awake looking through my door at the moonlight, when Caroline stepped quietly in. She was naked, she came over and knelt beside me. I think she thought I was asleep. She began very gently to pull the sheet off my naked body. In the gone days, I had often wanted to sleep with Caroline, but she had always brushed me off with 'some other time', but now? Love her as I did, in this lost world little desire rose in me.

'Caroline, I don't think I can . . .' I began.

'Can't you?' she said, almost angrily. 'Well, I can.' She wrenched the sheet away, placed her hands on my shoulder and then ran them suddenly down my body to my testicles and penis, which she squeezed gently but firmly.

'Come on, David,' she said, 'together, work.'

'Work!' I said, startled, but she closed my mouth with hers and swung her body onto me, slid her hands under my buttocks and pressed her groin hard into mine.

Then when I began to try and take her, she suddenly pulled away and started to tease me.

'I thought you said you couldn't.'

'I can, I will.'

'Catch me, then,' and she twisted away from me and shot out through the door. I was after her in a flash, caught her on the beach and took her fiercely and finely there on the sand. As I came I suddenly thought: this is my first emission for nearly a year. She lay quiet for a moment and then pushing me off her, went and washed herself in the sea. She came back tossing the water out of her hair, looking fresh and mischievous.

'Well done, David, my love.' She kissed me gently on the lips and then walked steadily up the strand towards Burgesser's hut.

We soon realised that each night all four of us were sharing her favours. Yet I felt no real jealousy; I was so involved in my own affair with Caroline. If at first it was with her body alone that Caroline loved me, that was not so from then on. She reminded me of things we had done together, spoke of occasions when she'd watched me from a distance, told me how she'd always admired me and I believed her, for it seemed no flattery but a genuine deep long-lasting love for me which she was unveiling. She made me speak out loud in the night, saying she loved to hear my voice. She stroked my face, stared into my eyes saying, 'my love, my love, my love.' Each night she seemed more passionate, holding my head tight against her and protesting with her eyes, her lips and her voice, a wild love and demanding to be taken again and again.

Then she passed onto the next. I detected in her at this time some sort of strain which I did not fully understand. As she left at night she would almost groan, and by day she sat unnaturally still for hours, occasionally smoking a cigarette in rather a furtive fashion. She swam a lot, lay on the beach quite naked, burning herself a gorgeous brown and, of course, slept during the day. It was an odd relationship between the five of us. We usually avoided speaking to each other about it.

One day I was sitting under a tree in the late afternoon discussing leisurely with Van Thal (the animal man from Cambridge) the difficulties we were having cooking the whitebait which Rondight (the airline pilot) caught with such facility. Caroline came out of her hut and she walked down into the sea. We both followed her with our eyes.

'She's so gorgeous.' I spoke aloud about her.

'A corny remark but true,' commented Van Thal.

'Do you really think she loves any of us?' I asked.

'Of course she does. She loves us all, loves us all. The question is, do we really love her?'

'Love her? I adore her. But what more does she want?'

Van Thal was not a laughing man, he was just constantly happy, smiled a lot, but on this occasion he actually gave me a little low pitched chuckle. 'Very slow, David. A baby, of course. What any girl wants and what any man ought to be able to give her. The question is, can we? What do you know about infertility?' Van Thal always loved to display to me his great knowledge of medical research, as well as the

13

width of his reading within his own field. 'Rubenstein as long ago as 1951 claimed that it was psychogenically caused in four fifths of infertile women. But then do you think Caroline is sterile?'

'Certainly not.'

'Well then, what about us men? Do you think you ought to do our sperm counts?' Still chuckling to himself, he got up and walked across the sand to Caroline, who had just come out of the water. He started to talk to her, gently stroking the outer aspect of her upper arm and making her laugh with some absurd memory of the gone world.

REFERENCES:

Batesm J (1967) 'A Human Mid-Brain Preparation', as described by E. Gamper. *Dev. Med and Child. Neurol.* 9. Brit. Mef. J. (1967) editorial 'S.T.P. 3, 570

Cohen, M. M., Marinello, M. J., Back, N., (1967) 'Chromosomal damage in human leucocytes induced by lysergic acid diethylamide'. *Science* 155 1471 — 19

Felinghetti, L., (1955) 'Pictures of the Gone World' in *A Coney Island of the Mind*. San Francisco: City Lights

Joyce, C. R. B. (1966) in *New Horizons on Psychology*. Ed B. Foss. London: Pelican.

Moser, R. E. Mathews, C. N., (1967) 'Peptide Synthesis from Hydrogen Cyanide and Water'. *Nature* 215. 1230

LE MAGASIN DES GANTS

O N THURSDAY, JUNE 3RD 19– at 3 p.m., the Countess of Niort entered Le Magasin des Gants. It was in a side street off the rue de Rivoli and shop and side street have long disappeared, but it survives of course in her husband's most famous painting of his first period, *Le Magasin des Gants*, and at the time secured the shop a fame and a clientèle. To such a client, Madame herself came forward: 'What did the Countess require?' She required some short kid gloves, just to cover her hands, buttoning below the wrist. In this warm weather she needed such gloves when she walked, as she did in the afternoons with her dogs in the Bois, the gloves to protect the soft skin of her hands from the harsh leather of the dogs' leads.

Madame des Gants rolled her eyes in a gesture of irritation. She had, on this dull afternoon, just one other customer in her shop. A gamine who herself had described just such a glove as her most distinguished customer, required. The gamine was even now trying such gloves, which had been pulled out from a deep drawer and placed on the counter for her. 'This one,' said Madame, 'is inspecting such gloves, but we shall—will—wait, Countess.'

'No, no,' said the Countess, 'Mademoiselle and I can both look together.'

This last remark the gamine must have heard, but she did not look round, simply buried her head with an assenting nod and continued to attend to the gloves she was turning over in the box in front of her. But she recognised the presence of another by moving half a pace to the side so that the Countess could conveniently inspect the contents of the drawer. Presently, the Countess picked up a glove and drew it on to her left hand. The fingers were exactly the right length. The glove ended where her slim wrist started and was buttoned lightly there at the wrist with a pearl. The Countess extended her hand to her left and away from her, flexed and extended her fingers with pleasure and reached out with her right hand for the second glove of the pair in the drawer.

Her right hand encountered the bare flesh of the left hand of the gamine. She turned towards her and saw at once that the girl had drawn on a right-hand glove, surely the mate of the one she had on, her hand fitting the right hand as tightly and as well as its partner fitted her. Then her eyes looked into the face of the girl and she saw the long ash-blonde hair to the shoulders, the deep grey eyes which stared intensely and held her gaze mutely for an astonishing period of time. Afterwards the Countess was aware it had only been seconds that they had gazed at each other, but it seemed an age, for Cecile de Niort thought that she had found, at last, the long lost Candida. But then realised at once that Candida by now would be thirty-eight, thirty-nine, whereas this girl, although identical to the memory she held of Candida, was younger, a mere twenty to twenty-two. Candida's daughter perhaps, except would Candida have had daughters?

Cecile Vincennes, as she then was, had been the most brilliant girl at her convent school. Her father's fortune (somewhat dubiously amassed during the Empire in sales of military material), from which he donated generously to the convent, assured her success with the nuns. Her long red hair always meticulously groomed, her athletic figure (she rode beautifully) made her unrivalled among her compatriots and her professors were astonished by the breadth of her reading, her ability at maths and the cool way she disputed with them about the ancient philosophers. Money, beauty, brains, what else would such a girl want.

Cecile knew, of course, she was admired, but exercised great control over her own responses. She was actually rather shy and tended to be quiet when her friends talked loudly of their families, their ambitions and their own perceived abilities. The young girls adored Cecile; she was aware that several modelled themselves on her, but none watched her more carefully than the young Candida. Candida chose to show her devotion in little acts of which Cecile was alone aware. Her thick nightdress was laid out on the bed for her, small gifts such as a mint would appear hidden in the folds, and when she was working, Candida would come and enquire if there was a book she needed to be fetched from the library, and begged to be allowed to carry out any such chores.

When Candida had first paid attention to Cecile, she had been an undeveloped 13-year-old, but by the time Cecile was to leave the convent, Candida had matured physically. She wore that long ash-blonde hair cut to the same length as Cecile's. She had the same cool manner, not talking much, but looking at you with her grey eyes: long intense glances, which Cecile thought had some message she could not fathom.

The day came when Cecile was to leave the convent. There had been certain ceremonies at which, of course, she had been awarded the chief prizes and now she had come to her small cell to close her box, adjust her hair, put on her hat and prepare to depart in the coach which would take her to catch the Paris train. Candida had appeared in the doorway and Cecile had smiled at her, and Candida spoke in her deep contralto voice: 'You know I love you.'

Cecile thought that maybe she should pat her cheek and say 'there, there, child,' but then she looked at Candida and saw this woman, mature like herself, full-grown and standing looking her straight in the eyes, and she could think of nothing to say, and felt suddenly a strange excitement she had never before experienced. Then Candida spoke again: 'I would like to embrace you.' Then Cecile smiled and reached out her hands, which had been adjusting the hair at the nape of her neck; not exactly opening her arms, but holding them apart so Candida could embrace her. Candida took her in her arms, held her tight, her whole body touching her, her face at first held off, looking at her, and then pressed her lips against Cecile's lips and tipped her tongue into Cecile's mouth, running it along Cecile's lips and pushing forward so that the tongues met. Cecile found herself hot, and as Candida released her, her breath for a moment came in short gasps. Candida looked at her and said: 'Find me again,' turned and left the room.

Well, she had tried—but not soon enough, not soon enough. By the time—it was six or seven years later—she returned to the convent, visiting the sisters, bearing gifts and asking oblique questions about her old companions, all traces of Candida seemed to have disappeared. 'She was a poor one that one, Countess.' There seemed no record even of her address and Cecile had to conceal the passion which overwhelmed her as she remembered that look, that kiss. But she had been too alarmed to react to that look at once, and then in any event there had been her passion—yes— passion, and marriage to the young, handsome artist Henri de Niort.

Henri could never remember a time when he had not liked to draw. 'Always drawing, that one,' he could hear the voices of his aunts when he was six, maybe seven. Not that he was unobliging, he did what was required of him. He learnt to ride, he learnt to shoot, to dress well. At school he attended, and if his professors thought him somewhat abstracted, he did enough to satisfy them and his father whilst he actually pondered how one could record on paper that shifting left eye of his Latin Master.

But there came a point when he was sixteen or seventeen when he announced to his father that he wished to become an artist. He wanted to go to Paris and take classes there. That was, in his father's view, not something a young French aristocrat did and he positively forbade it. But luck was on Henri's side; his father precipitately died and Henri found himself a Count and his own master. His mother had always adored this only child and she placed no obstacles in his way. Indeed, she did more. Although supremely uninterested in painting, she recalled that she had a distant cousin or some such, curiously enough also a Henri, and whom she heard had somewhat of a reputation as an artist. Shortly Henri found himself being welcomed with warmth and gusto in Paris by Toulouse-Lautrec.

Lautrec advised the young man to work in the studio of a Mr Grampian; indeed, recommended him there, then welcomed him to cafés, bars and clubs where he himself was such a recognised figure. Often one would see the short, bearded Lautrec sitting with his tall, fair young cousin. A curious pair, people said, but they shared this interest in what they saw. They shared other interests, also. Niort drank his fill beside his friend and if he was a little more restrained, people thought (wrongly) that in time he might become the drunkard that Lautrec was.

In one way Lautrec perhaps felt he failed; his young companion was never persuaded to have those close relationships which Lautrec attempted with the girls who were around him. From somewhere Henri had acquired romantic notions: he did not wish to indulge casually, he wanted to fall passionately in love and indulge his strong sexual feelings with a woman who would respond because of a passion and a love which she felt for him. Time passed and he remained celibate.

But his painting progressed. He observed Lautrec's interest in those companions of the bar and café and he thought himself that there were others who worked in Paris. He began a series of famous sketches of porters and workers in Les Halles. He sought out the poor shop girls to paint, and then one day greatly daring, persuaded Madame at the Magasin des Gants to sit for him between two counters of her shop, adorned as they were with gloves on artificial hands and arms. She herself sat, stretching out her own hands towards the artist and staring at them with a force that made one realise that for this lady gloves had replaced all other passions. Later he painted a whole series of pictures of the shopkeepers of Paris, but it was this painting, exhibited at the Orangerie, which attracted such attention and began the career which led to his reputation as one of the great Post-Impressionists.

If the younger Henri had borrowed from his older cousin some notions which had led him to the content of his paintings, the paintings themselves borrowed nothing from Lautrec. Not for Niort the free flowing line and the open space of a Lautrec. No, he was concerned minutely and passionately with detail, the very stitching of a glove, the hairs that sprouted from Madame des Gants' unfortunate mole. And his colour—those greys, suddenly, sharply contrasting with a brightness which led a cynical critic to say that the colours of Niort's palette were like those of the parrot. All this led to the celebrated attention given to him at his first exhibition.

Elated by the success of this first major public showing, Henri proceeded, as he always dutifully did in the summer, to join his mother in the country. But that summer was to prove special. His mother had written him that an old, recently widowed friend would be joining them with her beautiful young daughter, Cecile. Henri shrugged mentally at this obvious match-making. Indeed, he found that Adolphus, with whom he shared a studio, had met the girl: beautiful, but cold and mathematical. Henri left Paris reluctantly, saying he would be back within the month.

There was a curve of body, a firm thigh thrusting through the skirt: was that what caught his attention first? He couldn't say, because she rose and looked at him with those green-hazel eyes starting out of that face framed by that long red hair. Despite himself, he was fascinated. She spoke in a deep voice, and began to ask almost at once, fresh from Paris as he was, what he thought of the new novel that Mr Proust was publishing: the intellectual, as Adolphus had warned him, brilliant, beautiful and cold. Yet he found himself that night, and many subsequent nights, wondering how he could turn the conversation to express his desire and feeling for Cecile.

Every afternoon, the two widowed ladies set off for a drive in a carriage and every afternoon, Cecile and Henri walked or rode in the woods and grounds of the estate. They discussed first their families, the way they had lived as children. They discussed how one should live one's life and, greatly daring, Henri had asked how a woman should live, how the lives of sexes differed. Cecile had insisted on the equality of the sexes, the need for women to play as active a part in society as men and not to give up intellectual interests and activities. Henri politely agreed. They walked on afternoon after afternoon.

One such afternoon they came to the end of a ride, well concealed, within the woods, where there was an old eighteenth century well with a charming canopy. Henri sat on the low wall of the well and Cecile sat on the grass at his feet, spreading her skirt around her. That day she was wearing a costume designed to mimic the uniform of a hussar; it was in green with looped gold braid across the breast. The light sleeves ended at the wrist, but over it she wore long gloves which buttoned all the way up to the elbow. As she sat there she undid the buttons on each arm and slowly drew off the gloves and laid them across her skirt. Her slender bare wrists were exposed and, at the same time, she gently bent her head forward and backward, allowing her long hair to fall forward either side of her shoulders so that Henri could see the pair of muscles at the back of her neck. They seemed to him like the twin wrists that she had bared.

He placed his hand on her neck below the hairline and began gently to stroke her there. She wriggled back towards him with a sign so that he increased the vigour of his movements, running his fingers into her hair. To his astonishment, she began to pant and with a sudden convulsive movement, she tore open the tunic which fell aside revealing to him that she was naked underneath it.

It was not tristesse, Henri thought, but a detachment which came to one post-coitally. A detachment which left one disinterested in the events which had just taken place. He moved back from Cecile, who lay naked on the grass below

LE MAGASIN DES GANTS

him. She was still panting, her head arched, her eyes closed. He looked at her belly and that point where hair to the mound stopped and bare skin spread away. And then there was the curve where the red hair swept between her legs and darkened. Would it be possible to paint that? The colour of the skin itself was so complex: not white, not pink, not grey, but some subtle amalgam of all three and more colours. And then the red hair bursting up from that skin bringing a fresh colour and contour. Could one paint that? Cecile, opening her eyes fully and looking at his bare body, saw this intense gaze and interpreted it immediately as a sign of a renewal of his passion for her. That was soon aroused.

The house that the Count and Countess established became one of the most celebrated salons of that epoch, and Parisian memoirs of the time easily satisfy the curious as to who attended which dinners. They had two children who seemed to be born with an elegance and grace which allowed them to live contentedly in their parents' house. Those serious conversations before their marriage about what one should do with one's life troubled them somewhat. Henri, of course, had his work, his painting, his studio, where he went every day and worked. How they did work, those Impressionists and Post-Impressionists. Roomfuls of them in museums all over the world. Henri travelled too to other cities, the famous series from Brussels, the provincial French cities, the lives of the streets and markets he made his own.

The travels of course filled those immortal sketchbooks which now sell for such sensational sums. Because Niort was not a painter who completed his work on site—no, he returned to his studio to set up his huge canvases and from his notebooks created his immortal pictures. On his marriage, Henri had thought that perhaps his studio would be part of, or an annex to his home, but no, Cecile didn't want that. His work was his affair; it was away from her that he laboured. He returned to her for his rest, his sustenance at night.

Cecile, of course, had no need to work, but she busied herself. When the children were young she became concerned with the lives of other less fortunate young children and the poverty in which they lived in Paris. This led her to some political leanings. We even catch a glimpse of her in my grandfather's diaries. Belfort Bax, an early Marxist, who frequently represented British Socialism abroad. Indeed, he chaired meetings of French Marxists. He records in his diaries an evening in a Paris café where, sitting somewhat at the fringe of the group, was the beautiful Countess, and he notes her presence and wonders whether she would ever become a true socialist.

But as her children grew older, she became more involved in what we now call the Woman's Movement. Later, when Mrs Pankhurst visited and spoke in Paris (her daughter Christabel was in hiding there), it was Cecile who introduced her. She despatched a wreath from her sister in Paris, which was displayed prominently on the coffin of Emily Wilding-Davison, the suffragette who threw herself under the King's horse. In the afternoon in the salon of her house, she and her friends sat endlessly discussing how the state of woman in the world might be changed.

Henri could not, and did not, disapprove of all this activity. He was proud of his wife's prominence. But he regretted that in those walks, those long talks before their mutual passion had unfolded, he had not taken time to explain his romantic notions of the way two people should live engulfed in each other. He thought that everything of his was hers. He wrote her name in all his books, he wished his clothes might be mingled with hers in the same drawers. He had thought of Cecile being with him as he travelled to paint, being in the studio and, of course, he thought of that flesh of hers he longed to paint. He wanted her to be independent but sharing all his plans and his intentions. But he realised uneasily after four or five years of marriage that this concept was hard to achieve. It was about this time too that in his Cecile's mind the images of Candida sprang before her. And one day she took the train and carriage to search unavailingly for her.

Henri and Cecile's passion persisted discreetly, but they no longer sprawled naked on the open grass.

At last Henri decided that he must try to paint flesh. So he took the simple step of hiring a model and thus entered the famous second period of his career, dominated by canvas after canvas of the nude. The first great painting, *The Disclosure (La Révélation)* caused, as everyone recalls, a sensation when it was exhibited. The girl bending forward so her face is invisible and the clothes she has let fall a hazy background of garment from which springs her luminous belly, thighs and magnificent mound of Venus. And famously she holds in her left hand a long glove, which for some incongruous reason, she has not yet dropped to the ground.

But what then of the gamine, the beautiful girl who so resembled Candida, whose hand was a perfect match for Cecile's and who was searching for the same gloves in the Magasin des Gants on that Thursday afternoon in June? The gamine was, of course, the model whose flesh Henri so ferociously painted day after day. She had recognised the Countess immediately in the mirror behind the counter, glancing up to see who was entering the shop. But the Countess did not know her.

She was a country girl who had come to Paris, as such girls did, to make her 'dot'. So that she could eventually return to the province, marry and set up some respectable bar which she could lord over. When an artist approached her and offered to pay her handsomely to model for him, she thought it was a more lucrative way of earning her living than the more traditional labours that such a girl took on. She was puzzled that at the end of the day, Henri tidied away his paints and made no attempt at any more intimate relationship. No, no, he indicated he was away home to his wife.

He was unfailingly kind to her and, indeed, paid her too well. He encouraged her to move from her single room to a little apartment he found for her. His reason was he simply wanted his model, whose body was so fine, who sat so still, to live easily so that she could encourage the work they did together. The gamine's puzzlement grew to pique. Why did this handsome man not make love to her? She took to dressing more carefully, her hair had more attention, she bought expensive scents, but all to no avail. And so she developed a jealousy and an anger for the woman who was his wife. Why did she, who did not wait bare for him so much of the day, enjoy intimacies with him that she was denied? She waited outside her house one day when Henri was away, to have a look at her rival.

Madame des Gants was in despair. There was only the one pair of gloves of that size in the shop. Both women insisted that the other should take away the present pair while they would wait for the duplicated pair, which Madame des Gants swore would arrive from the factory the next day. In the end it was clear Madame would have her way, and the Countess finally went away with the gloves, but insisting on acquiring the address of the gamine and begging that she might call in two days to see that the gloves had been delivered. And an appointment was duly made.

Cecile's custom was to ride on a Saturday afternoon. When her ride was over, she hurried over to her carriage so as to be driven to the address she had been given, and she ran up the stairs still carrying her whip and wearing her riding gloves. She rang the bell and the gamine opened the door immediately, wearing the second pair of little kid gloves which had been delivered, as Madame des Gants had promised, on the previous day. She smiled and beckoned her in. Cecile tore into the room, tore off her gloves and placed the whip on a chair. She walked breathlessly around the room, breathing deeply as if the room held fresher air than the street outside, and then threw herself onto a chaise longue looking up expectantly at the girl who was silently watching her. Cecile had planned to say something moderate, like that she found the girl adorable, but from her lips fell the hackneyed 'Je t'adore', and she gazed up eagerly at the gamine. The gamine looked back at her, looked at the chair with the whip and riding gloves, looked at this lady who was Cecile, Countess de Niort, wife to the artist Henri, Count Niort. She smiled down at Cecile and slowly took off the small kid gloves which fitted her so trimly and which were a product of that most excellent emporium, Le Magasin des Gants.

YOUR HANDS DO NOT
PERMIT AN ATTACHMENT

Indian women usually prefer not to shake hands; instead the appropriate gesture is the 'namasthe', a folding of hands, palms together, as in prayer.

—From *Hints To Businessmen*, British Overseas Trade Board.

'YOU CAN PRACTISE DESCRIBING the scenery,' you said, 'love,' as we parted. Knowing I intended to write lengthily of another country—a country we both now know—where the land, like indeed this land, is old with the trampling of men, so that their terraces have been made, much has been cultivated and peeping stone walls supporting well-ordered beds of vegetables, fruit, vines, remind one of the care that centuries have put into that land. Here. Where to start? The view from the aeroplane circling over Delhi in the early morning, the browns and the mists of the plain, the identification of small round shapes—the villages of India on the plain, the realisation that the mist was also smoke blowing across and rising from early morning fires brewing—what? Some type of breakfast I could only hope—something to start the day with.

But this description, these plains, these accounts of mountains bestriding the railways, these have all been done before. I am tracing not the landscape, but the writers—romantic, all of them, too, when it comes down to it —who have described those same visions, so those same crows alighting in similarly sinister pastures admired by Kipling, by Forster, by Scott—'Imagine then, a flat land-scape, dark for the moment, but even so conveying ... an idea of immensity and distance ...' that is the appropriately done landscape even preceding a story of rape and violence.

Or should I take you swiftly along the 'Marine lines', a name simply for a street now (what were 'lines'? I have never understood) and shall we wonder why most people walk in the road rather than on the dusty unpathed tracks at the side which are littered with trash, scraps of food, here an odd dead rat, leaves, broken jasmine flowers and, in front of the temple here with people, squatting in tight rows waiting for something—I think the gift of some food —and with families who live here, the fifteen-month-old toddler I notice specially because of the bright silver ban-gles he wears on his ankles and how today he is squawking as his mother bathes him, displaying that anachronism of a clean people in a dirty country. Shall you then join me as I pass by through the swept driveway of my hotel to my air-conditioned room and throw myself on my bed and, finding you for the moment insubstantial and absent, begin to dream of you?

You then are the landscape I find myself wishing to describe, the landscapes which obsess my mind, the thoughts of again staring into ... and noting again their colour hazel ... but wishing to penetrate beyond them to the thoughts you might be having about me and the pattern of our relationship because it too has its anachro-nisms. It would also, if it could, be very clean and tidy, but around us hang other meetings and matings from which we cannot escape so easily, we cannot rush up to an air-con-ditioned room, we cannot escape, even in the nights, intrusions of other responsibilities; so that our landscape too is peopled with disillusionments, not about ourselves but about our ability to stay on an even ground maintaining the great ranges of passion for each other which abound around us and which we could explore easily were we alone and not on some vast sub-continent of human life.

So much love for description—romantic of course—but as I said following those people into this landscape, what can one do? Yesterday I was climbing the Ghats; climbing not physically but in the chauffeur—I should say bearer-driven —car to attend a ceremony up on the plateau at no less a place than Poona except Poona is not the local way to pro-nounce it—'Poone' is correct. It's like Istanbul which all the local foreigners (maybe the natives too) call Stamboul. The Ghats are climbed by a road cut by the British engi-neers during the war to speed their lorries up from Bombay harbour over to their troops in the Eastern half of the coun-try. Now the road still carries lorries driven hectically non-stop by their drivers until they break down or crash, both of which are common, my driver S. informs me. The road itself has sections where half the width has been bro-ken up and left as huge lumps of stone and tarmac and is waiting and has been waiting months for repair.

The crashes are clearly sensational. The relic we see of one—a lorry balanced half over the precipice—is startling enough but S. explains that often they go right over because the drivers are tired, they drive 24 hours non-stop to make the money and then they get tired and for a moment their hands—and Sundhar lifts his hands in demonstration—their hands are detached and are no longer on the wheel and they are over the Ghats. There is the complication too of the passengers. Mostly these lorry men will crowd their cabs with travellers but nobody knows their names. When the lorries go over, there are these dead women in the cab and the question is: who are they? To whom are they attached? What was their place in this landscape?

So into Poona and yes we are staying as I forecast at the Turf Club. It actually looks out over the race course and in the racing season one can clearly walk with one's drink over the deep green grass to look directly over the rails at the horses as they gallop (in this heat, presumably gallop) by.

I am trying to avoid too much involvement in this country with all these servants but it is hard. I have picked up my small night bag and carried it firmly in to the reception desk but it is taken from me and as the clerk puts the key to my room down in front of me a slim brown hand insinuates itself under mine and takes it. I am not even to carry my key or unlock my room. They hasten round me and wish to turn on a bath for me and I have to gesticulate firmly with my hands raised up palms outward to get them to leave me alone in my room for some moments before I set forth to the ceremony I am to attend. I adjust my hair, sit for a moment and then walk down through the gauntlet of bearers who bob at me as I go past.

It is the sixtieth anniversary of this institution and no less a person than the great Mrs G. herself is there to attend the ceremony. We needn't ask whether it was the time when she was prime minister. I am wafted to V.I.P. front row seats and am embarrassed to find myself coming under the attention of press photographers. Soon a little group of musicians appear, a line of dignitaries is arrayed at the entrance to the marquee on our right and at precisely the stated time the grand lady sweeps in. She is ushered to the platform and as soon as she is comfortably settled in the

31

very centre of the dais, she looks up at us all and turning to every corner of the room she makes that gesture—the namasthe—to us all and we applaud and then we—all of us—sit down.

I'm not of course going to bore you with any elaborate details of what went on. The wrappings are different but all ceremonies are the same. They are rituals and must lack any content. We had some music to start with, jangly stuff, and I suspect a singer. Then there were various gift takings or givings which culminated in the principal guest pulling the strings so that a picture appeared of an elderly person who had done something to start this whole assembly off. Then of course the lady had to be allowed her speech and like all speeches by politicians it nicely convinced us of the correct course of her actions. There clearly were no alternatives.

None of that however is worth remembering—it was like, as I have said, any such ceremony in any country varying with the culture a bit, but a ceremony. There was however one image that remained at the end of the day which had some unique quality about it. As I had walked or been guided round to the front of the marquee I had been aware that this was by any standards a large tent but also that behind the three or four rows of VIP chairs the audience—and they were all girls—was packed very tight. Now the sides of the tent were open, I sat to the left of the platform, the great lady exited to her right into a car which drove slowly down the right-hand side of the tent and then swept away. And we all looked back across at the car as it moved away, and what we suddenly saw, spurting into the air, was a great army of slender, quite beautifully slender, bare arms on the ends of which waved hands—hands waving in farewell.

Sitting in a car one often does suffer in this landscape the intrusion of hands. This of course is worse if you are recognisably foreign. As your taxi halts for the lights, the small hands come in at the window and the word one has associated with the age of PC Wren is quite quietly but endlessly muttered 'Baksheesh'. The worst ones for me are the mothers with babies who they show you through the window pointing at the babies' mouths. The infants look moribund or even comatose: my friends explain to me that, not to worry, the babies are hired and then drugged with opium. Is that true, I wonder? Of course sometimes the obscenity of an illness, eyes pouring with pus, accompanying the hand makes the whole thing a bit more of a burden. 'If you give them something you encourage that way of life,' I'm told. Still I compromise and make one donation a day.

When you say 'No' there is of course no response, the hand may be clutching at you now, anyway keeps coming through the window. 'Baksheesh', is murmured on and on. The drivers never involve themselves on your behalf and it all terminates only when the lights change and you roar off looking round hastily to see if begging children escaped safely to the road side. Eddie is the only Indian I've met who gives them money and he immediately remarks that his wife tells him he ought not to. Between us on the front seat is a biscuit tin and by chance I touch it during the conversation and he, glancing down at my hand on the tin feels he must explain that 'It's for the dogs.' 'The dogs?' I query. 'They beg too,' he explains, 'and they look so wretched that I give them a biscuit.' This behaviour forces an anglicism from me, 'What a splendidly illogical piece of behaviour,' I say. Eddie laughs and the lights change.

Your hands are not obtruding into this landscape at the moment but before I go on to describe a dinner with a beautiful girl I will remind you of a remark you made rather atypically. You lost, as they say, your cool as I was leaving. 'Don't make love to anyone else,' you said suddenly . . . Whereas we have discussed what I have called an open relationship and the need to accept that one's lover will from time to time be moved to accommodate with physical love some other human being—indeed since you and I met you have told me of such an event—so that that statement slipped out from you. It was not intended to impose any control on me, it was simply slipping out a statement about your love for me. I liked it.

Nevertheless I did take this beautiful lady out for dinner. She was tall, light of skin and the locals could tell me exactly where she came from and what her family was like. She was named after a flower. I had discovered a restaurant on my own where the curries seemed good but which I realised too late had no licence to sell alcoholic drinks. As soon as we sat down my companion took over with the waiters and dishes began to appear before us. She with a neat hand scooped her rice into balls and ate. She encouraged me to do likewise but it was too long since I had eaten like that and I fell back with an apology to a fork; for me that was the neater way of eating.

We began discussing, of course, the country we were in —the absurdity for me who had only seen the top left hand corner of the map in a nation populated with more people than all Europe and speaking a greater number of tongues —but I was like all travellers, eagerly wanting to make some observations of my own to someone who would listen. I gave my first observation, the ineffectiveness of the sweepers; those men and women squatting on the streets, on stairways, in rooms, endless sweeping with those stupid little brushes that were barely an extension of an arm, hand and fingers and which constantly broke and as constantly failed to clean the surface, the landscape to which they were applied. Why didn't they get some decent brooms?

Faced with my tendency to talk of such practical details my adversary moved from these specifics to theory and I was soon immersed in a cloud of mild Marxism which I of course countered by trying to sway the talk back again to specifics, to people and of course, for me, their personal relationships. I mentioned my habit of making love and the girl opposite me looked up at me and said in her cool voice, 'It's the cream on the coffee.'

We had reached that stage now and that flash of eyes made me wish to advance our relationship further and it occurred to me that in another landscape I would have reached across the table at that point and touched her bare arm and sought to hold her hand but here in this restaurant with waiters hovering it was not to be done. So I had to content myself with a slow lingering walk back to our lodgings, fortunately near each other, our hands swinging separately at our sides, our eyes mostly looking down, mine darting nervously from side to side to contain the rats who scuffled at the roadside and occasionally seemed to threaten to run across our feet.

'So I kept myself for you.' Not exactly an act of dedication, more an inability to handle the customs of a country. But when I got in myself, my hands untouched, I did of course think of you and the way your hands reach out to me and was glad to be alone. Acts of dedication in the form of abstinence, I thought, are not alien to this culture and I thought of the religious accompaniment which must go with such acts although the form in this country was alien and unknown. So the next day I set out to see such acts and sought some caves; caves I had discovered were in fact ancient religious sites; one's imagination had littered the sub-continent with temples and these were to be found at the 'caves'.

Next day then I was sitting before a temple thinking of how you would behave in this landscape. It had been a long climb up to the temples and I had gone up fast. At first to try and throw off the attentions of the many would-be guides and then to try and indicate to them that I had not hurried to get away from them but that this was my normal hill climbing pace. So now I was sitting not recovering exactly but contemplating the little new temple built just outside the main old temple which was carved into the solid rock. The new temple, I found, was an active site of religious activity and acts of dedication.

Between me and the temple, a little trail of people appeared; a middle-aged woman accompanied by a companion who stood a little behind her and behind them both two young men who kept looking away as if they wished they were not involved. I noticed one had arms which hung down rather stiffly to his sides and then realised that was because he was holding by their legs a chicken in each hand. The woman was intoning some message to the temple and at some point the man suddenly threw the chickens up in the air clearly aiming to get them over the temple. One fell a bit short but the other thudded satisfactorily onto the roof. I had thought the birds dead as they had hung so immobile in his hands but they were not. After crashing on the roof that bird actually flew down and was soon joined by the other and they scattered off into the ancient monument pursued by an ancient ragged man (was he a priest?) and a boy who had been sitting quietly against the front of the temple but who now hurried to claim these gifts for their God.

Fearing that when they caught their prey I might witness their immediate despatch, I got down and set off along a path that straggled just under the crest of the cliff. I thought perhaps in a mile or so it would climb up and give me a view over the other side of the range on the south side of which the temple was embedded. An Indian preceded me by some 20 yards and I was careful not to catch him up, not wanting to have to attempt conversation. As I came round a corner I saw that he had paused and that on the ground in front of him a thick brown rope was writhing. The day was providing me with everything traditionally Indian—temples and snakes.

The man turned hastily and came back past me. He paused in front of me and pointed behind him and then wriggled his arm sinuously. Then he waved his arm, shook his head as he pointed behind and then pointed back up the path to the temple. I smiled, nodded and turned slowly to follow him not wishing to display unnatural haste, and there was no indication that the creature was pursuing us up the path. I strolled along attempting to appear casual as if my decision to turn round was not occasioned by the wildlife. Suddenly I came upon my temple party again. The lady this time was standing facing the cliff front and was addressing her remarks to a crack in the rock which I had noticed on the way past contained a withered bouquet of flowers. I tried to walk even more slowly to see what gift they would offer the crack but one of the young men looked at me and was clearly aware of my interest.

Later, in the small village below the temple I met them all again and the young man touched the 'leading' lady and pointed me out to her, clearly telling her that I had watched them at the 'crack'. I realised now that they were in the process of celebration and she came over bowing, smiling and laughing at me. She held out her right hand and I saw she was holding some powdered jellies; the youth took my right hand and pulled it towards the lady's indicating that I should take some and I guessed that a gift to a stranger could form part of their rituals. They waited while I took one and watched me eat it and then pressed more on me. I managed to refuse for the moment but as I walked through the village, looking at the rather dowdy curio shops, I kept meeting them and on each occasion felt obliged to take another of the sticky objects from a hand which, although a right hand, might not be as clean as its owner intended it to be.

There was an easy solution and that was to go down back to my waiting car and again to move fast so that the temple party could not catch me.

Going down the hill the willingness of that hand to offer me sweets impressed me with memories of the other hands to which I had been making offerings. Hands that reach out for me, secured me to them or hands that ever so gently kept me at times away. And what I've tried to explain is that if the hands reject you how can you expect what lies behind the hands to reach out to you? If you are incapable of sustaining and renewing a physical contact is there a possibility of another contact? And yet here I was hurrying away from hands that had offered me sweets.

S. had of course got our car under the one tree capable of providing any shade and he rose, his short greying hair, head bowing politely, and his face smiling politely and asking me, had I enjoyed it? 'Of course,' I replied, 'very much.' And we settled comfortably beside each other and set off to our next call. And I recalled how this dignified man had actually given a shout of pleasure when I pushed for a second time sweating out of the customs shed into his country and we had embraced, for a moment actually held each other in our arms. Perhaps I should have made more of an honest answer to his question about my visit to the temple. I could have replied with that peculiarly Indian gesture of the head, neither a nod or shake but a motion putting the head diagonally to one side and then the other conveying 'maybe', 'all right', 'let me think about it'. I stretched my arm to cool myself and it, my hand lying behind him on his seat but not forming an attachment between us.

So now I'll return to your landscape. You are kneeling before me and my hands are lying at the bottom of your spine either side of your backbone and as I trace that ridge up and allow my hands to spread out to your ribs I see that your back has something of the shape of India but your long slender arms are reaching back entwining round my legs to pull me to your head which lies up where Central Asia lies, where indeed they say all our civilisations blossomed. Your head cranes round towards me shattering that image of India, tearing it somehow as something redundant, something aside to which I have failed to make a connection while you are blossoming again and wishing me to move again and to reinforce the depths of our attachment.

SECONDS OUT OF THE RING

HENRY JONES BLINKED AND rubbed his eyes. He bent forward and fiddled with one of the knobs but the picture did not change. Indeed, as he bent forward, there was a close-up and the disagreeably close female pubis made him start back. He had not listened properly to the usually inane introduction bawled out from the middle of the ring by the man in the dinner jacket. And at his first glance at the screen, he had assumed that this was going to be one of those tiresome matches between women of which he so much disapproved. But as he settled down on the sofa with the whisky he'd collected he saw that this match really was going to be different. The girl—and she really was a girl too, not one of those stringy female fighters—the girl had nothing on. Not even those splendid laced-up rubber shoes that fighters wore and which Henry rather envied. The camera passed lovingly up her. It was at this point that Henry bent forward to adjust the set and at this point that he was so startled by this close-up of naked female loins. He couldn't help noticing as he hurried back onto the sofa that the hair which was black had been combed out instead of being pressed back flat against the skin—as with his wife, for example—it really was bushy. It caught the arc lights and shone in them, perhaps she had oiled it? By the time he looked again the camera was just moving off the naked and well-developed breasts over the bare shoulders and onto the face. He breathed a sigh of relief to be free of embarrassment and remarked to himself that the girl (with her shoulder-length black hair, prominent cheekbones, slender nose, bright eyes, etc.) was strikingly pretty.

'Oh! You and your old wrestling,' his wife's voice broke in. Henry stood up hastily so that he was between the screen and Debbie, his wife, who was standing at the door of their sitting room.

'Don't stay too long now, dear,' she went on.

'Er, no,' said Henry, eyeing her sadly. Same old bloody mug of Horlicks and faded hot-water bottle in its cover, it's that tickly knitted cover Mrs Pettigrew gave us the Christmas before last—'No. No, I shan't be long. I just thought I'd have a peek and see what was happening before I came up.'

'All right then dear, but it's gone eleven now.' Debbie wrapped her rather shabby dressing gown around her somewhat dumpy body and stumped out.

Henry flopped back again into his seat as the door shut. She'd knock on the bloody ceiling too if he didn't go up soon. Oh well, he glanced uninterested at the screen again and suddenly remembered but all seemed back to normal. A tall, chunky and not unhandsome man was just climbing through the ropes. He had a magnificent dark dressing gown with 'Hole in One' embroidered across the back. Strange for a wrestler, thought Henry. Then the man shrugged off the gown and Henry saw he was quite naked too.

The camera was giving him the same all-over treatment that the girl had received and Henry, slightly less startled now, was able to take in the commentator's soft burr, 'Well! Here is the great Alex Kennedy, as sexual a hunk of manhood as you're ever likely to meet. Tonight is his forty-third professional match. He hasn't lost in his last twenty matches and drawn only once in the famous disputed match with Lysenkova. Three or four have gone full distance but there's usually a submission to Alex. Ah! There are his genitals and, as you'll see, he's circumcised. Well,

I've no need to go over that well-known argument. Suffice to say that Alex swears by his circumcised one: he was telling me in the dressing room that it is not only in action that it's superior but he says it looks more attractive and excites the girls more. Ah!'

'Seconds out of the ring,' says another voice.

'I'm worried about Henry,' says Debbie Jones to Celia Johnson.

'Oh dear.'

'He works so hard, you know.'

'So does John.'

It was true that Henry always managed to bring home papers from the office. The evening had a sort of pattern to it. He got in 7.30 to 8.00 p.m. and in reply to a question would mutter, 'Very busy day again.'

'I'll have your supper on in a moment, dear, then.'

'No hurry,' Henry would say and he'd hasten off to the gin cupboard. Summoned to the table he'd sigh heavily as he sat down: not that it actually discouraged her talking but it did mean she didn't ask him to talk. She'd prattle away about the price of peas while he munched his way solidly through the meal. It was only after coffee that he permitted himself an almost affable remark.

'Well my dear, 'fraid I must go and get at those papers.'

'Could you leave it just one night?'

'Never do to get behind, old thing.'

And he'd trudge off into their other room and spread the papers out on the table. They were the same papers that he'd been bringing home for years. They came from the bottom drawer of the desk of a colleague who'd retired and Henry was supposed to be looking over them to see if there was anything important there. But everybody had forgotten them and what Henry actually did was to play a complicated word-game with them which he'd devised himself. You started with eight piles and tried to get them all into one pile. He always told Debbie his papers were confidential so she'd never looked at his pre-war letters and long out-dated insurance policies.

Actually, he was fairly bored with the game now (just as he was fairly bored with his job). What he relished about the papers was the chance to be alone. The chance to dream! He'd spread the papers, slump into his chair and out would come his pipe. It was difficult to say precisely what he dreamt about, probably mostly of being able to sit all day in a chair, smoke his pipe and dream. Round about eleven, when she'd gone up, he'd slip across and watch late-night television, hoping it would go on until she was asleep.

'Of course,' said his wife, 'he has got a position to keep up.'

As the referee drew his hands away, they went into a deep clinch. Their legs were working hard together but the camera closed up on their lips. Henry had never seen such a kiss! They seemed to be trying to eat each other. Suddenly the girl drew back and with some quick flick of her feet tripped the man onto his back. Then flung herself on him wriggling round into what Henry thought the most extraordinary position.

'How beautifully she went into that soixante—' said the commentator.

Saturday mornings, Henry played golf with John while their wives met up for a coffee and then joined 'the men' for a drink before lunch at the club. Henry didn't get a great deal of actual pleasure out of playing but there was the

43

vague pleasurable feeling that he was taking some exercise. He enjoyed the drink too and after the second round he and John got quite sociable. It was people that interested Henry; he used to say—

'Now take a man like Smith. Been with his firm for thirty years and then he does a bloody silly thing like . . .' or John, who was a stockbroker, would say—

'Did you hear about Joe Brown. Put a big batch into United Profit Making but forgot to countersign the certificate. They wouldn't let him claim, oh no, dropped the lot.'

'Really.'

They had a good lunch on Saturdays. Afterwards Henry liked to settle down on the sofa with a pipe which mostly took him through till teatime. Mrs Jones washed up alone. Saturday night they always had a television supper and the box stayed on until the programmes ended. But Mrs Jones, who always got up at seven o'clock, used to begin to nod off at half past ten. She was always hoping that on Saturday night at least he'd come up to bed a little earlier but, as he explained, the late-night programmes on Saturdays were particularly good and anyway he needed to unwind a bit. Once, years ago, Debbie had said playfully—

'Why don't you unwind with me?' But Henry had looked at her so stonily that she'd never tried a remark like that again.

'Well, I don't see this match going the full length,' said the commentator.

'No,' said his sidekick, 'I think we'll get a submission soon.'

As far as Henry could work out (after all, the rules of ordinary wrestling were bad enough) any sort of hold was allowed except that ultimate one and the aim of the match seemed to be to induce a state approaching orgasm in one's opponent so that he or she begged to be taken. Clearly both the fighters were approaching this state, panting with excitement from the start of the round, despite the efforts of their seconds who had poured cold water on them, slapped their faces and read them old-fashioned religious tracts during the half-minute interval.

The girl shut her eyes through most of the round and had gone all passive. She concentrated on trying to keep his hands off her breasts which seemed to send her more than even genital touches. The man, on the other hand, was so excited that he hadn't the sense to realise this and was throwing her round almost savagely, groaning at her, 'Come on, let me take you.' Every now and then, the girl would push him wearily away and say unconvincingly, 'I don't want you,' and then pull him thankfully towards her again moaning desperately, 'But you want me.'

The fans, of course, were wild by this time, and the commentator's voice had gone all shrill. Suddenly there it was.

'Ah, submission,' the commentator moaned. Henry bent forward and switched off the set with a sigh.

When the programme was over, Henry waited for a moment or two. Often she knocked on the floor as soon as she heard the noise stop. If she did that he'd stay down and read or something, but tonight there was silence. That usually meant she was asleep. Henry crept upstairs quietly but when he got into the bedroom there she was sitting up and reading.

'Hullo,' she said, smiling shyly at him. She was wearing, he noticed, the black nightie he'd given her in a moment of affection three Christmases ago. He gave her a sort of half nod and undressed with his usual slow clumsy movements. Then he laboriously climbed into the ring.

BEDS

Half our days we pass in the shadow of earth; and the brother of death exacteth a third part of our lives. A good part of our sleep is peered out with visions and fantastical objects, werein we are confessedly deceived! That some have never dreamed is as improbable as that some have never laughed, that children dream not the first half year; that men dream not isnsome countries, with may more, are unto me sick men's dreams; dreams out of the ivory gate, and visions before midnight.

—Sir Thomas Browne's *Religio Medici and Urn Burial.*

ONE SUNDAY MORNING after the war, I was lying in my bed when I heard my father shuffle across the landing into the bathroom which lay just behind my bedhead. Before he turned on the water (so did he mean me to hear?) he muttered, 'Bloody Bitch—gone to church—and taken the car with her.' Unfair, unfair, how could she have got to church—a good five miles away—without the car. But as I lay there I knew that this was no comment on my mother's church-going or on her early rising, but rather on her not lying down—beside him—in a bed.

It was many years since it had been established that my parents had separate bedrooms: it went back to the days before the war when we lived in quite a different house and where my parents had that big room with its own bathroom and those big twin beds pushed together. But then also, across that landing, they had, or rather my father had his 'dressing room'. Some mornings I remembered seeing him shuffle over there. They were Victoria born, were both

46

my parents, so that room in itself was not surprising in a middle-class house—only the use it was put to.

I had graduated (this again way back before the war) to my own adult bed and separate bedroom. There I lay then in what seemed a huge bed which you could crawl into and totally disappear. I awoke one hot summer night to find I had disappeared in this way and lay buried, sweating, half suffocated and a bit panicked till I pushed my way out beyond the bed and out of my bedroom and into the passage—not crying but making enough noise to rouse my unsleeping father who emerged—this in the middle of the night—not from the bedroom but from the dressing room.

'I got stuck in my bed,' I said.

'It's the middle of the night,' he replied and took me back and, no doubt, put me back into my own bed.

I was sufficiently curious in the morning to ask my mother—my father long gone to work—why he was banished to that (very high, I remember) bed in his dressing room. My mother, startled, made some reply:

'Oh, my snoring'—she did snore—'keeps him awake.' But even then at the age of five or six I knew that the noises of the night do not flush a lover from his bed. Thence to the next house where two beds were still kept in one room but one of them, I fear, was never used and then the move to a final home where there were those two clear separate bedrooms each with its single bed.

But with the war my father sent me to safety. I would have preferred of course to stay, having no fears of wars, but plenty of strangers, strange rooms and strange beds. I was away then to the single iron-framed beds favoured by the poorer sorts of boarding schools. There were people, of course, who would share them with you.

'I say, Ursula,' begged her chum, Lesley, 'may I come into your bed, so that we can talk without disturbing the others!' And talk they did: suddenly Lesley's strong impulsive arms were wound tightly round her and Lesley's voice with a break in it exclaimed: 'Don't be such a dear idiot! Of course you're wanted especially by me . . .' These friendly schoolgirl beds are not like the ones I encountered, although we crossed indeed from one bed to another and when we lay in rows with partitions between the beds, strong young male hands would force their way under the partition to reach out strongly for one's body, one's flesh. I reached back from my single bed yearning for something more than sleep; not blaming but wondering if, in dismissing me, my father had wanted me to experience the nature of separation.

Alone, I have spent many years in beds—single beds— and have slept alone in double beds, even in king-sized beds, bean bag beds, couchettes, air mattresses, sofas—my feet in a chair, and the places one has lain which don't really justify the name bed, viz, a mat on a concrete floor of a school in Heraklion. South African prisoners (so Breytenbach tells us) call this 'sleeping camel' because the skin on the hips eventually becomes calloused. Helen Suzman may have been responsible for getting these wretched prisoners beds and the prisoners referred to her as Auntie but in a way she was and is more of a father to them.

There have been beds too, which I have slept in, which themselves have made some attempt to provide you with something more than sleep. Like the bed in the Chicago motel which when fed a quarter would shake and rattle like a washing machine so you awoke tossed and spun. Or beds accidentally shared with friends who had not purposed to share the night together. Peter and Edwin each lay sleepless on the outer sides of their bed for fear they might touch but Tony when I shared with him (used no doubt to sharing on Cheetham Hill) lay untroubled beside me. I lay rigid, sleepless, till dozing at last I was awoken by his movement and tensed again as he rose up beside me, slid open the window above my head and peed out of it into the night. Alone I *prefer* the narrow beds like that which Wellington campaigned in and which, as a lady commented to the great man, were so slender one could not twist in them.

'When it's time to turn over, it's time to turn out.'

To the days then (which I think my father sought) when the beds I slept in were shared. The rushed hopes of youth when we lay on a bed so narrow that I slept with an arm propped on the ground to stop me falling out while you lay compressed against the wall. And the secret beds we have shared; that night when we entered the wrong room and I hid behind the door while you encountered the ancient lady who told you the shape and state of her heart.

And there have been those occasions when seeking a shared bed, at the penultimate hour one has been dismissed with a 'I'm sorry love, but I can't make love in snatched hours in a narrow bed'. That sort of dismissal leaves one creeping out into the night forced to trace a path through dim corridors, past stiff fire doors to a narrow room with again a narrow bed on which one is forced to lie without the succour of love or friendship.

(One could here, in parenthesis, talk of other beds. Beds of Alabaster, beds of Agate, beds of Antimony. All the rare beds. Or again perhaps the more mundane beds — asparagus beds, watercress beds (down by the riverside), once a whole bed of radishes. My father liked these vegetable beds well enough, would even work at them a little, but liked best to clean them out and burn their waste on a slow fire he tended all day. Forgetting botanical beds we could together view the bed on which an ancient printer will lay his lead to set up the text of this tale.

And then there is the issue of historical beds. I have already animadverted on the beds of the Good King Rene of Provence who, if one believes history, even lay chastely beside the Maid of Orleans. Or I could invoke the famed lovers' beds and record how the gods abandoned Anthony there: At midnight, when suddenly you hear an invisible procession going by with exquisite music, voices, don't mourn your luck that's failing now ... Or I could even record something in song: 'By night on my bed I sought him whom my soul loveth.'

There have been solidly purchased beds—double beds, not those wooden twins my father must have ordered from somewhere like the Army and Navy Stores around 1930, but first a cheap wrought-iron model with a flock mattress. It stood square but not firm, the mattress moulded itself into lumps and the soft metal legs slowly sprayed out and slowly from the heights we were lowered to the ground.

Those beds which do duty in the day as couches we seemed to collect. The first was an unwanted gift, a subsidiary part slid out from under the main strings and a doubled-out mattress attempted to correct the difference in height between the two sections, but it failed and we lay on the two platforms one above the other arguing the night away as to who was the superior. That all might be described as pillow talk. But when my father came to stay it was the bed on which he—alone of course—was accommodated.

There is the noise of beds—unique to the bed and not

its occupants. One drummed its headboard against the wall and to stop its deathly rattles and to prevent it boring a hole in the wall it was eventually covered with layers of cloth. Those beds made with curiously coiled strings spoke a language of their own twisting their way into your conscience and your conversation. There was a great continental bed that spoke in the middle of the night like a big bass drum as a board snapped and we were once more deposited on the ground. There were melodious beds and there were mournful beds, there were beds which spoke with a sound of menace.

You could try moving beds around. I noticed you doing this. Changing lovers you moved your bed. It used to stand just inside the door so you could rush in and flop on it and grab some instant sleep. Although, as you said you needed your sleep, you changed its position and hid it behind the door. It became a Surreptitious Bed which one could slink onto unobserved and without, you said, making the slightest change in one's lifestyle. It was just somewhere to hole out until the weather changed. You could go further and actually move the beds from one room to another, changing the purpose of the rooms and the purpose of the beds.

All the time you could say the beds were getting harder. There was indeed the hard-up bed bought at an Oxfam shop but it had a twisted spring and had to go in the end like all the others. So it was time to go for something that made no attempt to massage the limbs or assuage the spirit. It was not a bed to sink into but rather something on which the surgeon could operate. It was a bed that certainly gave nothing to you but rather that took what it could. Still it was a bed on which two could lie—at a pinch.

All this time while I speculated in beds, my father was

getting older. Did he speculate or conceive of all the uses there were to a bed? To be sure he was still a light sleeper: something disturbed him in the night—maybe he was up still searching for an errant son. He would rise, don a few clothes and then begin to tramp around the house. When one roused oneself and came to him, he would accept that it was the night, return to his bedroom, strip off the old cardigan he had put on over his nightclothes and seem to settle himself peacefully enough for sleep again. But if one lay down oneself one would be disturbed in five minutes when he rose again to pursue his nightly marching. It was easier in the end to leave him circling the house than to try and explain to him the real purposes of the night.

My friend Taner took a personal interest in these nocturnal wanderings of my father and saw them as a desire to be back in the drudgery of his working days in an office. Was it true he saw them as nothing else but commuting on slow trains and that he woke to the Bradshaw and began to dress for a past journey? It was a possible explanation but I doubt myself if that was what the old man was really looking for on those nocturnal ramblings.

Came the night, came the day when he rose no longer from his bed but lay washed up beyond the tides which had carried him to and fro for so many years. The doctor called daily, not attempting too strenuously to oppose the course of these events, but merely to ease him with some minor remedies.

'Why don't you,' he said to Mother, 'offer him a little brandy?' This she did, choosing to give him the little sips he was prepared to take not from a glass but from an egg-cup—perhaps there was some obscure symbolism in that. My father had always been proud of his ability to speak French and liked to borrow phrases from that language but even I was startled when on one of those latter days he replied to a kindly enquiry about his well-being from the doctor with the phrase 'Comme ci, comme ça'. He turned his head a little restlessly but then stilled and closed his eyes on us. He seemed at last to lie there at rest, knowing that there was a need for sleep.

FIVE HOURS TO VESPERS

A MAN HAS PLACED a hat on the shelving where we want to put our drinks. It is a bowler hat and I can tell, without giving it a friendly rap, that it is one of those hard solid hats — hats which their owners believe impart them some stability, some status in our society. Its owner is red in the face and talking to a lady who is also wearing a hat and all I remember of her face is that it is white — heavily powdered — in contrast to that of her companion. The man glances at us from time to time — wishing, I think, that he was able to persuade his lady to treat him as my lady is treating me.

My lady asked me to take her coat as soon as we had got into the crowded bar and wedged our way across into our corner which is somehow between the food bar and a coat stand now overladen with our coats as well as, no doubt, the coats of the hat owner and the powdered lady. That pair are beyond the coat stand and we find the only place to put our glasses is around on their side of the coat stand just in front of the bowler hat. My lady is not wanting to hold her drink as she wants to slide her hands under my jacket against my shirt while at the same time leaning her whole body against me.

My lady's dress is denim and all down the front there are brown buttons, each rather more than a hand's width apart; I could slip my hand between a pair of them easily. I would love to do that but have to content myself with saying (which is true) that I would like to undo all the buttons. To which I get the good reply, 'I wish you could.' And we

54

look at each other eye to eye and we laugh and then, Lady, you make another remark, something very personal about my behaviour—why you like me—and suddenly my laughter stops because I can feel tears coming, I lean my head and I breathe deeply saying nothing until I have swallowed. I am suffering/enjoying all the hysteria that love engenders.

It is an hour we have. I glanced at my watch as we came in. We would like to be alone in a small room with a bed but we live in a large city, a conurbation—the urbanation extends not only to the intricacies of the streets, alleys—through which I walk daily—courts, yards, precincts, small parks, pools, ornamental ponds, fountains, palaces, all that bit but also to elaborate human structures—wives—lives intricately connected, work schedules, Marxist memories, analytical counselling, patterns of people woven so together that when two move out of their parts they cannot simply align themselves together, they must creep to another part of the city, find a crowded hour and stand there at the bar for the time they are allowed. The time allowed is still (I repeat) only one hour. I glance down at my watch to detect that most of it has gone.

The thought of the hour we are having, in which both of us have told the other more of the past, let the other probe into details—'I swore I'd never tell you that,' my lady said—has entirely eliminated reservations we had each developed during two days of separation in our week-old affair and we are both astounded by the way we feel—yes, this thought, this feel is a good one and thinking this I remember that quotation about a glorious hour. 'One crowded hour of glorious life is worth an age without a name.' When I was fifteen I used to walk round repeating this hackneyed couplet to myself and I tell my lady this. She understands the glory of the hour but is puzzled by my interest in the quotation: so I glance again at my watch and read this time the date — March 30th, Monday March 30th.

March 30th, the date is an anniversary of not an ordinary but of a certain extraordinary Easter Monday. It is the anniversary of the Sicilian Vespers. The anniversary of that day in twelve hundred and eighty-two when the Angevins of Sicily were slaughtered by the inhabitants as the bell rang out for Vespers. These then are the elements in this story — two lovers, a bar, an hour, a day and the bloody end of the Angevin rule in Sicily. What is it that has brought these elements together (here now, always)?

In 1282, Charles of Anjou (so Runciman tells us) was the greatest ruler in Europe — and wanted to become even greater. The Popes had nominated him King of the Scillies and with that nomination and his power base in France, he had dominated the Italian peninsular. Now with two rivals — an indolent southerner, Manfred, and Conradin, a youth from the north of only 16 who Charles had despicably executed. Both rivals then disposed of, Charles stood poised for his greatest adventures. He was aiming for Constantinople; with the blessing of a Pope who had excommunicated an Emperor of the East, Charles's ships, troops, were ready to set out to make him an Emperor of a recombined East and West Roman Empire.

What, my lady, has this to do with you? It is, my love, that you are an Angevin Princess; because you bring with you to me — as did all such brides — wide territories, unrestricted provinces which you lay at my feet. You want to give me you say all your extensive possessions and you flaunt them at me and I take them. I take you for what you are. You are already a Princess of Provence (you told me so yourself) but your dowry includes Toulouse, Carcassonne, Anjou. If our relationship was arranged, was a formal one —which indeed it was—no accident brought us together —yet you yourself are saying to me—'I give it all to you, not only that which I bring in dowry but those deepest parts of myself, my homelands, my own Provence, the seat of my soul which I open to you. Take all I offer you.'

From Anjou comes your sternness, because those Angevin ladies (look at the wife of that later King René) they were stern, they could rule. They gave you your tall forehead, your long nose on which one of those medieval helmets could rest. So that René's wife (when he lay in prison) took ship and claimed for him his kingdoms of Naples and Cicily. Anjou gives you that coolness, that assurance I've commented on, that quiet efficiency (I am not well organised), that structuring you wish to give to my life, that ease with which when you tell me of some of your past sadnesses, some of your pains, you can say to me (at the point of cradling me in your arms) 'I can look after myself'.

But your hazel eyes, leaning against me here beside the bar, belie that confidence. You tell me 'I'll open myself to you' and I think then of those areas behind your battlements, behind the fabled towers of Carcassonne, behind the complexities of turret and wall to the intricacies within you. The small square we came across where we sat outside, where the children, of course, ate ice cream, where you calmly concluded several different analyses of my nature. Taking away from me confused ideas, jumbled computer print-outs, all the mad medley of medieval town planning, you come back with it all sorted out for me, arranged for me to understand like a magic map. Your intellect is busy rearranging my brain.

Which brings me to your hillsides, the orchards of

Provence, in winter there are oranges, tangerines and clementines, the fruit trees, the wine yards, the Popperin pears into whose long firm bodies we laid our teeth, those full red grapes we made into wine. (Of the wines of Provence, best known, because it is one of the very few which travels, is Châteauneuf-du-Pape . . .) The hills and valleys where intimacy takes place, the terraced landscape of your mind where tucked under your hauteur hide (and I saw him by your bed when you invited me there) those poems, the Portuguese Love Songs by the South American genius. You asked me to read one while you cut the cheese and I sipped at that wine. From the seas that border Provence one looks up to great mountains stretching away to columns of snow in the sky—your long white thighs which I tell you about because you seem unaware of them as I compare their beauties to the Alps and then the bower between—the soft garden of ease in your Provence.

Meanwhile another man is disturbing us. I have insisted you eat because you told me that since we met you had lost five pounds—unable to eat because of me you say. I beg you, my Lady, eat. Quiche Lorraine (of course) and we are nibbling occasionally, you still directing your whole long body against my side and this suited man is suddenly saying, 'Excuse me, can I reach round you for the mustard.' There on the shelf is a large pot of mustard. We are the sole repositories of mustard in the whole restaurant and, interrupting us again, he is back to return the pot and ask me for a knife which somehow again we lock away from him. And I have to detach myself from you and, as he apologises for disturbing me, I have to say—'Not at all, not at all.'

I am back therefore with the time against me telling you about the glorious hour and how I, as a youth, had thought to myself that the glorious hour was what one should aim for. And that I had those sorts of ambitions, not exactly the ambitions of Charles of Anjou, not the simple ambitions of megalomania, the urge to rule, to have power, all that. No, there is a difference between me and Charles (surely more than one), but I wanted as a child to achieve something, I knew not what, but I wanted to have honour and glory, I wanted renown. And I could have all that now, I simply have to state that you are my Queen, that all your wide demesnes have come to me and my fame and glory are assured.

Be wary though. At this moment as I approach my glory, behind me, as behind Charles, lie forgotten enemies. Here is Runciman: is this a description of me? '(They) had drunk well and were carefree and soon they treated the younger women with a familiarity that outraged the (Sicilians).' What followed? 'He drew his knife and fell on D. and stabbed him to death. The Frenchmen rushed up to avenge their comrade and suddenly found themselves surrounded by a host of furious Sicilians, all armed with daggers and swords. Not one of the Frenchmen survived. At that moment the bell of the Church of the Holy Spirit and all the churches of the city began to ring for Vespers.'

I am sorry that these are unhappy thoughts nor can I fully explain our complex relationship with the Sicilians — perhaps it is this bar. I push you back from me a little and buy you another drink. Shaking my head from side to side I decide I must look away and some of the grey people in the bar begin to acquire faces. I used to come here years ago with Peter and Gavin. It was a quiet place where we would sit upstairs with cheese, a bottle or two of wine and discuss poetry of course and women. Although both can of course do either, Gavin is particularly good on the women, Peter (probably) his peer at poetry.

It comes to me now that in the intervening years this bar has changed, a different breed of men have taken it over. The hat—an absurd relic of an outworn age—is symptomatic of these men of business who have invaded my private bar. Or were they always here and I the invader? I notice now that they are men of conformity, they like an ordered and orderly society. They want people to live in the traditional ways, they are not catholic. If we were very brave you and I might want to burst out of this world but these men have long knives concealed under their coats. But you are tough when I moan and say 'this is awful', you reject that, you cheer me. 'It is not,' you say. You give my love fibre, you encourage me to persist.

The quotation will recur to me later in the day and I suddenly realise that familiar as it is, I do not know its source. Usually it's Shakespeare again when I'm missing a quotation but this time it's someone new who I can't even immediately trace in my companion. The author is Thomas Osbert Mordaunt and there is just the one quotation from him so, apart from the title of his books, all I gain from my search is a couplet which precedes the two famous ones. 'Sound, sound the clarion, fill the fife'—the sort of martial stuff I expected, but then: 'Throughout the *sensual* world proclaim, one crowded hour of glorious life is worth an age without a name.'

That is something. It is not these men in this bar who I should be telling about us. It is another world, a sensual world where there are people who will want to know about us. I am telling them now. I have now, my lady, to help you on with your grey coat which like all your other appurtenances I have learned to love. (I was amazed when you were dismissive of a jacket you wear.) The hour has been

extended and we must leave. The choices I sought in childhood are over. They never existed. I shall never live in an
age without a name. You and I, my lady, are fated for some
glorious life and there are, as yet, five hours to Vespers.

(The quotations come from Sir Steven Runciman's brilliant 'The Sicilian
Vespers' published by Cambridge University Press 1962.)

IN THE SEVENTH HEAVEN

SOMETHING WAS CHANGED. Moggs knew that and stirred in his chair. He had been digesting the pre-fabricated steak and kidney pie which Flo had heated up for rather too long in the oven. He brought his hand away from his forehead, which it was supporting, and struck down at the arm of his chair. It was an action which had irritated his wife for many years. He told her such pounding helped his thought, but it was really a purposeless substitute which helped pass the time.

This very action alerted him still more for he immediately observed that he was no longer in his own worn, beaten-up, chintzy chair, but in something far more ornate and grand—although quite as comfortable. The arm ended in a carved wooden head of some sort; it could be a leopard or, perhaps, more likely, a lion. Brass nails tacked what looked like leather to the arms and, touching the seat, it felt like leather, too. He had a definite feeling, almost knowledge, that this chair had a very much higher back than the one to which he was accustomed. Glancing up, he saw that he was right—the back extended up two foot six, not three foot. He hadn't worked thirty years in the building trade for nothing, he was good at judging short distances. The top was square and he deduced that the leather was wrapped and tacked onto supports which were probably made of, say, about a three-inch timber.

Particularly striking was the design which somebody had worked in gold on the leather of the top half of the chair back. The design was a twelve-pointed crown, surrounded, almost illuminated, by stars. The result was quite startling and Moggs realised that if he sat up straight the crown would be perched just above his head and he would look quite regal.

Turning his attention away from the chair, he saw at once that he was no longer in the parlour at 303 the Harrow Road (Albert Moggs and Sons—Builders and Decorators—not that there were any sons). The walls had expanded or just gone and his eyes were first arrested by a ring of grey figures, a little below him and none nearer than twenty yards. He imagined his chair was encircled and, glancing over his right and left shoulders he saw, not only that that was so, but that there was a figure flanking him on either side of his chair. Turning hastily forward again—not wishing to stare impudently at people so close to him—he looked slowly round the ring of faces in front of him.

A little to his right, a particular cast of feature attracted him—a rather thin face, but nice brown smiley eyes. The eyes met his and he smiled back. He made a sort of half-gesture and she (he was sure it was a she) ran lightly up to him. He made room for her beside him on his handsome chair. He turned to have a good lustful look at her, but was held back for a moment by the thought of the watching multitude. He made another vague gesture and, with a thrill of pleasure, watched them all disappear in a twinkling. Good on you, Moggsie!

The chair dipped back slowly like those aeroplane seats and converted, readily enough, to a good solid bed. Moggs was able to concentrate on the girl. When stripped of her grey tunic, she proved to be lacking certain basic feminine equipment and also to have certain unnecessary accessories (wings, 3 prs, shoulders, buttocks, ankles). Moggs struck at these sharply with an open hand and they fell off. He remembered as a small boy reading about knights being defaced or something and having their spurs knocked off. It must have been just like that.

Turning her over onto her back he looked at her front. It was smooth, flat and hairless from neck to thigh—not a protuberance anywhere. A word came up into his mind which crosswords used to define it—epicene, that was it, epicene. He looked at her face, brown hair, dog-like eyes adoring. She looked at him.

'Do what you like to me.'

Nothing to do at the moment, old girl, thought Moggs, but given courage, thrust his hands on her flat chest and mounded up large firm conical breasts. Nipples too, Moggsie. Leave it to me, old stager. Permanently a little erect these will be, he thought, as he rolled them between thumb and forefinger.

Then the groin. First to muss up some matted thick-but-short curly hair. Lovely! Then, with the middle finger, rapidly to open up a lip, out and in. This is it, Moggsie, this is it.

Squatting back on his haunches, he watched her lying there, quite quiet except for the occasional convulsive pant. My God, he thought, she did it just right, right with me she was; I wonder if she'd . . . And he looked down at her and knew she would do those things he'd heard about in the army (fellatio, cunnilingus), but never dared ask Flo—Gawd!

Then, suddenly, he couldn't be bothered; not exactly a revulsion with the whole thing, but the knowledge that it was too easy. She would do it, without any persuading at all. He came off his haunches into a sitting position and began to wonder what was the most difficult thing he tried to do and knew right away. His hobby—nuclear physics. It was a strange one for a small-time builder (and decorator), but he had to have a hobby of some sort. Otherwise Florence was always getting at him with small jobs round the house or the garden. What he wanted was a small room to himself. So he'd fitted one up, told her he was going to study. He chose physics because he'd done it one term at school and the master said in his report that he showed aptitude (couldn't remember his face actually). Flo couldn't but be impressed.

Teach Yourself Nuclear Physics was very difficult stuff. He didn't actually read it much, had it on the table. Then he'd found out the names of a couple of specialist magazines. He got them regularly though he couldn't understand them at all. He just read the news section. That was quite interesting. Harvard, for instance, had just built a new neutron accelerator.

That was it! Moggs realised he was sitting in his leather chair again. He'd just float down, he was sure he could, and ask one of the boffins to show him over the thing. He almost set off, but pulled up with a jolt. He was just thinking—ask him what's what—when he realised he knew, knew—all the answers! Quick as a flash, he could visualise the whole thing three-dimensionally and in model sections. He even knew how it worked too, which was more than they did down there.

Moggs sat back thunderstruck, worried, uneasy. He turned to look at his side-kicks. The one on the right put him off a bit, wearing some sort of shiny tin—oh, yes, armour—and with that sword, standing there just as if he was a statue. So he turned to the one on his left, who was a grey, tunic-clad type and asked him, 'Who am I?'

Gabriel smiled at his master's perpetual inventiveness. 'Why my Lord . . .'

The boredom—again.

YOU, ME AND THE LOVE-LIGHT IN YOUR EYES

THIS STORY IS SIMPLY one of those corny old love stories about almost touches, glances across crowded rooms and failed consummation. And, if you do not like corny old love stories, you need not bother to read on. The whole episode began, as you will recall, at some sort of gathering or function which we had both been forced to attend. I had been sat next to a foreigner from, I would say now, Serbo-Croatia and he was explaining to me how his interest in music had been stimulated in Vienna before the war and relating this, in some obscure way, to the even obscurer functions of that gathering in which we (you and I) were involved. Looking up I saw you looking down attending to your soup but, for a subliminal moment, our eyes had just met. I knew immediately that this had been no casual study of a stranger but a call of recognition which left one excited, a little surprised and, even now, many years after one had first met such a message, confused as to how to meet the demands which the look implied.

The Language of the Eyes I now understand and whereas the first time I'd received such a signal I'd been confused on two counts—the first the lady's meaning and second how to act—I now realised that, even when the message came over clear and at once, action remained as difficult and impossible as it had been before. Still that dingy hall where we were eating was filled, and I say this with all sincerity, with a feeling of light bringing back memories of that first encounter made under the bright Aegean sun. To transfer us from this urban to that absurdly romantic setting, may seem to you pointless and I can only reply that it is ourselves and not our settings which determine the future course of events.

To return to our earlier adventure, I had left my parents and was totally on my own for the first time. I was not lonely exactly—there were plenty of people around who I could talk to—but I was aware of a total separation from all previous human contact and consequently I felt free to start any relationship in any way I liked, in a way that might be totally different to my pre-separation behaviour. Clad as a student, hampered by a rucksack, I'd travelled all down Europe and taken a boat at Brindisi. The boat was full and the steerage quarters filthy so that one felt sweaty and unclean the whole time. I had sat on the stern rail, holding onto the flag pole. Doing this one got dirtier still because smuts blew back onto one's bare body but a faint wind did somewhat offset the dirt and sweat no longer trickled down one's side from one's armpits. I suppose I looked almost relaxed and then you (then) came.

You lay down on the thick anchor rope coiled beneath me. Your body angled away from mine but right under me and I, who'd been, as I say, almost relaxed, found nowhere to look and so I looked down and you tilted your head but as it rolled backwards you allowed your eyes to close so that I had no message from you then. My eye was drawn down inevitably, now that your head no longer obscured my vision, to your long body—the traditional cleavage, the tight yellow bathing dress (bikinis were not being worn that year or you would certainly have been wearing one), to the tops of your legs and the junction of thigh with body. Here the costume was so tightly pressed into the groin that, bursting around the edges of the dress, one could distinctly see, two, three, maybe a dozen each side, curly hairs peeping from their place of concealment. What was consoling to me then was to realise, for the first time, that the hairs there on a lady were the same colour and bore the same rich promise as the hairs which hung down from your bent-back head which you shook from time to time gently to allow the air to circulate through them.

I started to sweat again. You didn't stay very long. You got up and walked away from me, not jerking your hips from side to side in a too deliberately provocative manner but nevertheless moving them from side to side and making one aware of the muscles around the thighs, the tensions that could be built up there and the sustained energy centred in your groin but growing out of the whole beautiful potential of each part of your body.

That was an experience in itself but it would have been the end of it had it not been for the 'look'—the love-light I've called it. It was the next day, we arrived late in Athens. It was near midday, very hot again and I was bent a little with my rucksack on my back, lugging my sleeping bag and trying to keep my place in the fight to the gang plank. You, of course, were carrying nothing—some poor German was struggling with his and with your luggage. Come to think of it, I believe you had something with you—a bag or a little reticule on your arm—because something broke the symmetry of your arms, the right bent in towards your body but the left was long bare. You were wearing, I recall, a green blouse and I think a yellow skirt but I may be confusing that with the bathing dress. Any rate three steps down the plank (which was I should explain parallel to the ship and not at right angles to it), you paused and looked straight up at me. This was no subliminal message, no half glance. This was the whole thing—the message in toto.

I've mentioned that I didn't know what it meant at the time. I remember saying to myself, 'She wants to know me again so she's looking hard at me.' But realising that this was an internal excuse and that there was much more to it than that. But action, that was the problem. I made feeble efforts to get to the gang-plank faster but it was hopeless. When finally I stood on the quayside (first time on Greek soil or rather concrete) she was gone. All I knew was that that wasn't the end. We were going to be given some opportunity to do something with the situation and I had to be ready to seize whatever I was presented with.

I don't want to suggest here that 'fate' or anything laughable like that was involved. She was going to provide the situation. That wasn't difficult. In those very early fifties there were very few people going to Greece—too soon after their war—and we were bound to meet up somewhere. We were bound to be visiting the same well-known sites, planning to reach Sunion as the sun set or being up at dawn to see the sun rise over the Crelan Mesara, attempting to wrench out of other people's objets trouvés some unique experiences for ourselves. The place reeked of meetings—that was what it was for—not a chance to fight with destiny, fate or something obscure but actually to meet touch see and feel things from the present.

About ten days later I was on the same or a similar boat sailing along the northern coast of Crete. We had gone first to Candia and were now on our way to Heraklion. Four or five hours it took. It was the mid-afternoon and most people were asleep. I was sitting on a bench under the awning looking out sleepily at the sparse coastline and thinking hazily of the Minoan ships and all that bit about the maritime empire that they were supposed to have defended from their great city at Knossos. Or at least I imagine I had some such equally romantic notion in my mind. I was certainly not thinking of action. I was not thinking of people in general or women in particular and I had not got, as one well might have on such a warm lazy afternoon, the slightest sign of an erection.

I didn't even know that she was on the boat. She must have spotted me. She came suddenly along the sidewalk and sat quickly down beside me. There was about two feet between us and I was already leaning that way. My hand was on the bench, my fingers flexed at the last two joints and my knuckles pointing towards her. She too looked out at the Cretan coast but she put her hand down, not to lean on, merely to rest it there and to allow it to creep along towards my own. Finally it was brought to a halt firmly touching my own hand. Then she did look at me. And I was forced to turn and look at her. There she was and this complex look I'm trying to describe too. It said everything and finally it said, 'Your move.'

I did nothing. I can give all the traditional excuses. My tongue clove to the roof of my mouth. I thought she was French (she was, as it happened, but her English was excellent and, in any event, my French is passable). You may imagine too that I had moral or even religious scruples about sexual relations. I hadn't. And at that stage simple sex was not being offered although it would surely have come to that. My religious beliefs had gone some years before when a parson tried to tell me what a soul was and, as for moral beliefs (whatever they are), I simply believed that people should contact each other by any means possible. I believed in any kind of love. I still do as a matter of fact.

No this was a simple straight failure. It was a failure of

the spirit if you like. But then I don't know what the spirit is either. It was that I was just incapable of responding to the challenge—the stimulus—before me. My education, upbringing had sucked from me my innate human curiosity and left me so dry and arid that I cowered away from the very possibility of traumatic exciting human activity. I said I'll stay a spectator, I'll preserve the status quo, there's no hurry, this can happen again later when I'm ready for it, just now I'm—well, yes really frightened, I'll let it go. These were my excuses and all I've learnt in between is that each act as a spectator makes it easier to stay that way but that without involvement the mind decays, the body atrophies.

So now here I am and you giving me the love-light across the room. You may think that this is all just a bit of special pleading. In truth things have changed for me. I have my own family now—a wife who I love (whatever that means), children, and what's more, inescapable commitments. Things to do tomorrow which must be done. But what I'm concerned with now is to force myself into this action. Drag myself through the business of arrangements (which I must make this time). Reach eventually the stage when you and I are together and when I begin to study your golden hair, look closely into your love-lit eyes, indulge indeed in all the saga of a love story. But then, as I said, you may not like corny old love stories and, if that is the case, do not bother to read on.

BIBLE STORIES 3 / SONG OF SOLOMON

The song of songs, which is Solomon's
Let him kiss me with the kisses of his mouth;
For thy love is better than wine
Thy name is an ointment poured forth.

Not bloody likely. Starts trying to chat me up before I'd even has a glass—little does he know me.

'I'm Solomon,'—a young f-ing banker I suppose and, by God he is! I'm Solomon' starts to tell me all about his bonuses: 'Only been at it four or five years and I'm up to a hundred grand this year—see I understand money, can move about too. Fast R.B.S. like that.'

Suppose he's as rich as Croesus (who ever the fuck he was) and he wants to prove it to me—take me out: 'I can afford to take you to real class.' Guess he's had a few to come out with such a crass approach. 'Bankers,' I say, 'you're all bloody bastards—out for money for yourselves.'

'We're not, we're bloody not. We're the people who make the world go round.' 'Tick, tock,' I say. 'One day you're going to get a shock.' You may be Solomon in all your glory, but I'm the preacher Vanity of Vanities I say, and out I go in high fettle. He doesn't even know the preacher is in Ecclesiastes

Talk about looking daggers. Well all I'm doing is to offer a free meal. Well maybe there will be an afterwards but I don't say anything about that. Tell her what I do but she goes for me before I've got a word out, I just say something about the job and she's down my throat as if I was Satan himself. Preaching at me as if I'm something evil. Look I am come to great estate and have gotten more wisdom than all they that have been before me in Jerusalem— yes, my heart has great experience of wisdom and knowledge. Well, she's not having any of my wisdom, after all, I am Solomon. But I'm not getting anything but knives driven into me – I would cause thee to drink of spiced wine. I charge you O Daughter of Jerusalem that you stir me not up.

The coals thereof are coals of fire. Yes, let her remember the day of darkness.

3.
Party Time

Well they must have
had parties then, can't
have all been waiting
around in vineyards for
something to happen. The
daughters of Jerusalem had
pretty wild
times.

It was all in the vineyard.
And vineyards are good
places to dance if you can
step round the vines.

No, you'll never
know my name
but here's
something not
in the authorised
version—that's
me dead
centre,
don't
you
like
the hair?
And what's that
lad doing bounding
about? I'm
chucking him a
ball when I
recognise him.
Why, it's

Solomon.

Solomon,' I say,   'what's happened to
the suit?' 'That   was dressing up for the Queen of Sheba. I got
sacked—made   redundant, they call it. You were right about
those bloody bosses   of mine, and it's great.' 'I'm thinking to
myself who is this   that cometh/out of the wilderness/like
pillars of smoke/   Pertained with myrrh and frankincense,/
with all the powders of   the merchant? (Was a bit of a
drug scene.) So I shout at him: 'What are you up to then?'

'Solomon!' I shout, 'You can't be doing tango. Not way back then. Anyway, it's the wrong continent.' 'Ah, forget that, the old Lord was about everywhere, so while he was setting up all this myrrh and incense stuff in the Middle East He was out there in Argentina setting up the tango. I bet He had a good time flitting from continent to continent.

'That's why I'm concentrating on the tango—it's back to basics for me. I help Anthony Howell—you know, the poet—he's running tango classes for old people and while I'm shouting he steps, and putting them through their paces he's reading out loud to them from "The Song of Solomon". And he fits the rhythms together perfectly.' 'Where's he doing all this?'

'All over the world, of course, God's on our side so He's universal. Come along, we have a great time.' 'Maybe I will—sounds better than an expensive dinner.'

But actually of course, it was back to basics, and here we are actually airborne.

I am coming to my garden/ my sister, my spouse

I have gathered my myrrh with my spice

Eaten my honeycomb with my honey,/ Drunk my wine with milk.

Eat, O friends, drink abundantly,   O beloved.

I sleep, but my head waketh/ It is the voice of my beloved
I rose up to open to my beloved

Well, I knew you'd want the details but they didn't put in his flying sofa. I don't know where he got that from, but we were up, up and singing. I can't tell where we're going to come down, but it's in Solomon's Song.

76

JOURNEYINGS (A SLIGHTLY ROMANTIC TALE)

IN MY DREAM, A GODDESS (but it was not you, my love) came to me and laid beside me a girdle and bade me wake and take it to bind the winged horse to my command. And I awoke and beside me was the golden band the virgin queen had unloosed and I arose and went to the altar and there knelt the horse; so with a gentle hand I girt him, bestrode him and we were away—gently—gently to you, my love. So it was a good dream, love. But, dispersing with the real morning and a real wakening with the journey uncompleted and you away from me.

Your dream lacked this magic, it was full of practical things. You were packing your bags, filling them with clothes you wished to wear in my presence. A blue silken shirt you'd bought, scents to spray your body, a robe in case we chose to rise from our naked bed and walk at night. Gifts for me, nectar from the North—a strong golden liquid to refresh us, a loose cotton blouse from the East, sandals from Greece. All this and more you had and, suddenly, you had to pack and be off and your case contracted, lost its size, it overflowed and you were not ready, you were flying down the stairs telling a car to wait but it could not and it was gone.

And you awoke, tossed, turned to reach me but knew I was far off in another land awaiting you, so you swore to yourself no cabman would keep you from me and so you slept again ... to find you had a willing driver and you were slipping through damp dawnlit streets and your driver was asking: 'Where are you for my lady,' and you were shyly telling him, 'I'm meeting a friend in . . .' and he was saying, 'You're off to your lover, miss. I see it in your eyes. We must not be late.' But your kindly driver soon had you stuck in traffic jams, huge lorries crawled forward in front of you, brick-laden trucks prevented him overtaking, your car finally halted and your driver turned you out and told you to run. Your ran but looking back saw your sadness in his eyes as he waved knowing your meeting with me was going to be missed. And then you woke again hot, anxious, awaiting and wanting.

Tonight I should be flying high. But my airliner is delayed at take off. I am having a free meal in an airport for these delays. They have issued instructions they say for further wine to be brought and I drink deep, to help my dreaming, of when this flight will end and in my fancies, I can see you there ready to welcome me. I know so well the soft words spoken, the gentle hand pulling me to your couch but the wine will take me no further and I climb reluctantly to my plane to allow myself to be strapped in and I cannot decide now if I am flying away or towards you.

It is towards midnight we touch down and I know where it is. Reykjavik. Halfway between the New World and the Old World. Where are you? I know not. I stumble out and with me now there are three or four companions and we crouch down on small stools around an upturned barrel and we are playing cards. Why am I playing cards, love, when I should be with you? I am numbed by the mishaps of my journey and I have determined to stop my imaginings so I have talked to a crew man demanding his pack of cards which he gives me. It is Icelandic, the court cards are Nordic Heroes, Frega the ice queen with pale grey eyes stares at me—another virgin enticing me to her sterile bed away from your fertile bounds. I lose a trick.

What of you this night, lover? You have clambered aboard a train. The guards are foreign, you can hear dimly the names of stations through the closed window (which you cannot open). You are undecided as to whether this is your connection but the train pulls out; soon it is dark, the rain begins to fall, the lights are faint and the names of the towns when you halt are poorly writ in Cyrillic script but you are travelling still my love, you have set out, I know that and you mean to arrive.

Where shall we meet then in these dreams, love? Shall we have got to the South and the sun and when you arrive will I be there in a red car with the doors open, stumbling as I hasten towards you? And before we can stop and embrace we will be aboard, the petrol will be running out and it will be hurrying you towards your next unlikely destination. Your cases will have been crammed in the boot, your eyes are filling with tears as you recall all the gifts that you have not yet had time to give me.

But maybe you are there first, love, awaiting me in some backstreet hotel. I have confused the directions and am buying a street map to try and sort out my way. I cannot understand the currency and when I obtain my ticket on their monorailed subway systems, automatic gates bar me from the train. So I am late struggling down the street, fearing you will have gone, searching frantically for the name of the hotel in my pockets, entering the wrong one, finding it at last, confusing the desk clerk with my importunities, but she dials a room number and says to me . . . 'Madam will descend.' An antique elevator beside me begins to move and rattle. Who will push open the double gilt doors when it finally grates onto the ground floor?

All this anxiety, these fears we have now about travelling
—the news of automobile smashes in the newspaper—the
feverish listening for information about the airline strikes
—the irritation with the lisping radio announcers whose
weather check suggests the boat will not sail. The rising
price of crude oil, the blow-outs depriving us of energies—
the wasted years when fuel was simply filling the tank—
the lack of comprehension of how one can possibly travel
anywhere and remotely hope to arrive. All this surely my
love is because of our concerns about the end of this particular journey, the need to know whether and when we
have met last, whether we shall be able to travel together
and where we shall take each other. 'What shall I do with
you?' you ask. 'What are you going to do with me, my lady?'

Will you on our journeys take me into a church dedi-
cated to a virgin saint whose girdle quietened a monster?
And will we stand together amazed at her gilt images and
will we wander apart and shall I lose you among the pillars,
the side altars, broken levels of chancel and nave and shall
I catch sight of you as you stand looking up at the vaulted
roof so that the sun from a high window catches you and I
can see your hand, the fingers stretched wide held across
your thighs? And will you turn then and walk and buy a tall
candle and light it and place it on the altar? Shall I then
intrude and ask you for whom that passion flower is burning?

Or shall we wander together through a gatehouse dispersing some coins to a peasant and walking down
between an avenue of plane trees catch sight of a ruined
castle? Pass across the drawbridge and pacing the yard
come to a high keep its tall walls still standing with the
breach repaired—repaired by du Guesclin the man who
made it those many years ago. And shall we stand and look

up through those vacant floors past the corbels which sup-
ported the missing roof and will you turn then and pray to
me that we should have such a château where we could
shut ourselves and stay? Put an end to those ceaseless
searchings, those journeyings towards a destination where
we can love and linger.

It might be that we would be away from all traces of
building and of man. We have driven off down a side lane,
the car is tucked unobtrusively under a tree. We would be
slipping quietly into the wood. Brushing through the scrub
—oak with the wild thyme crushed beneath our feet—
would you take hold of me and lead me on, deeper into
that forest and, where the pines stood thickest would you
press me to the earth? And would you let your long hands
work on my body, bring your passions to me so that I would
beg to let us stay there and let this journeying cease?

Or we might be slipping indeed into a palace wondering
if there was a room for us and finding it was as if we were
expected, a graceful girl would lead us to a room and when
we were showered, with fresh clothes we would slip down
the stairs and slide quietly into the dining hall. But they
would come and lead us to a dais by a high window where
we could look at the rain-swept hills and see through a
storm the lights in the valley below us. And when we had
drunk of the wine of that country would they lead us to our
room and would you then pull me by the hand towards you
and hold me there through a long night saying, 'I love it
when your arms enfold me tight.'

If our journeyings reach these goals my lady love, shall
we there want to set out afresh? Will we decide that time
too must travel for us? Will we commit ourselves to longer
journeyings? Will we search for things to bind ourselves
together? Will we be able to face the strange travellers who

we shall meet who will try to disturb us and turn us separately away from each other towards new faces and new worlds?

Or shall we, love, reject them and decide we shall stay always with each other? Will you then at last enter my dreams? Will I realise as I bridle my horse that the girdle I slip over his great head is your girdle. As I mount him will I see you standing by the way so that I may, as the great beast moves forward, reach forward and, as you slip your robe from you, lift your beauty up so that together Pegasus will bear us away? Shall we then pour up against the light, and do strange deeds upon the clouds?

A TRIP TO DUBLIN

(for the two Neils)

HE TOOK A TAXI from the airport to the school and spent an hour with the head. He wasn't sure why she'd wanted him to come but the department had been very keen.

'Contacts with the Irish . . . and then you can go to that study day in the afternoon.'

But the head didn't really seem to know why he'd come either and she had to go off to a meeting. There was the usual showing around—talk about this and that.

'We really want you to talk to Jim—does the interfacing for the children.'

'Where is Jim?'

'Back after lunch.'

The head reappeared and took him to lunch—rather nice steamed pudding after rather nasty dried-up fish. He kept being offered glasses of water. He never drank water except when he had school dinners. Two staff to talk to. Been there years. He tried not to think 'institutionalised'. The head took him to the staff room for coffee.

'You'll have to wait and see Jim, I have to teach.'

Half past one he was alone there. No Jim but there was his own coat, there was his usual heavy bag. He grabbed them, shot out the front door, ran into the street. And ran fifty yards. Then he pulled up . . . How was he to get away? He didn't really know where he was. He only knew the centre bit of Dublin and the walk to the bus terminal or airport. But the meeting was near here. A bus? He saw a bus stop and stood at it. And—glory of glories—a taxi driving down the almost trafficless suburban street.

The conference centre was in some new development. He got into a complex of new shops, English many of them, and a French Connection. He went into one and tried on a jacket or two. But he had enough jackets. There was an escalator up to the second floor and then a carpeted floor. A notice 'All Ireland Childhood Disability Conference'. There were two girls sitting at a table. One had bright red hair and what he called clear skin. No freckles. She jumped up, came round the table and shook his hand. She was wearing faded jeans. Very tight into the crotch.

'How nice you came. It's lovely to see you again.'

He'd never seen her before but he shook her hand. She had a lovely Irish lilt to her voice.

'It's Doctor . . .' she said to her colleague. She gave him a label and one of those silly plastic folders.

'They're only just started—the afternoon session.' The entry door—silly—was at the front so he had to slink into the second row. What was the meeting about anyway? He opened the folder and slid out the programme. It was a two-day meeting. Was today Thursday or Friday? He finally worked out the speaker's name. He never knew what he was really talking about. Some time later it was tea. He'd 'been'—perhaps he could go now? He wandered back into the conference room. There was his chair with his coat and plastic folder on it. But where was his briefcase? He thought he'd tucked it behind his legs but it wasn't there . . . He went out to the front table. The red-haired girl was gone but the mousy-haired one was sitting there.

'Your briefcase,' she said. 'Did you have it when you

came? Nothing's been handed in.' He couldn't remember.

'Maybe you left it in the taxi,' she said. Perhaps he had. His briefcase. Everything was in it, his diary, all that urgent work for the plane. His notes on liability. His dictaphone full of messages to himself.

'We could ring the taxi company,' she suggested.

'Yes, yes,' he said. She picked up the phone.

'Engaged. They're always engaged. You could go out there.'

'Out where?'

'To the taxi terminal. It's not far.'

'How will I get there?'

'There's always a line of cars on the front outside.'

He hurried down and, yes, there was a row of cars, not taxis; nevertheless the first one pushed the passenger door open and a hand beckoned. He got in and before he could say where he wanted to go they shot off, pulling firmly out into the traffic.

'I want the taxi terminal,' he said. He got his legs settled straight under the dashboard and then turned to look at this determined driver. To his astonishment he found it was the red-haired girl.

'Hullo,' he said. 'It's you.'

'I know it's me,' she said.

'I've lost my briefcase,' he said.

'I know.' How did she know, he thought; but perhaps it would be rude to ask. He contented himself with saying, 'I want to go to the taxi terminal.'

'I know,' she said.

There was a lot of traffic. They edged forward but then the lights went red on them. He turned to say it was kind of her to drive him but she turned more vigorously, took his head in both her hands and kissed him hard on the mouth. Then turned swiftly back to her driving. Should he ask where they had met before? It seemed somehow rude with the level of intimacy that was being offered.

'Won't they need you at the conference?'

'They've all come now and Angela can cope.' But what was her name? They were driving now through what seemed a poor part of the city. Late forties single-storied houses. Then the road actually ceased to be made up and they came to a square or more neatly a circle of what was intended to be grass but was mostly earth. On the far side he could see a small hut, around it a bevy of taxis was parked. They pulled up by what seemed to be a half-built hall of some sort. There was a breeze block wall up to about eight feet but above that there was just canvas. The effect was rather like a big top at the circus only smaller and more scruffy. Loud music emanated from inside.

They got out and stood in front of the entrance which was simply a canvas flap you could push aside. In front of it there was a table with a notice: 'Disco. Entrance £2.50.' A youth stood jingling some money; he didn't seem very interested in them. Suddenly his girl bounced through the flap without any attempt at payment. He ran through after her.

She was crouched down looking around her. There might be about thirty people there so the space was by no means full. But it was only mid-afternoon. The group were on a dais in front with coloured lights flooded over them and then round to the audience. Along the right-hand wall were tables with glasses; above them a sign saying 'drinks'. Two desultory barmen were half listening to the group.

She bounced again over to the bar. As she moved something caught his eye as it fell from her back pocket. He bent forward to pick up a little bundle of green punts wrapped round some coins. He put them in his pocket and looked to join her at the bar but she moved again and stood in front of the group looking and maybe listening. He came beside and she took his had. It was too noisy to talk—and it wasn't his sort of music.

They squeezed hands together. She was looking at the group and he was looking at her. Then she turned and smiled and putted him firmly over to the left-hand wall pushing him back against the wall, took his head again in firm hands and tongue-kissed him hard. His hands were on her buttocks in those good tight jeans. He slid them round the front and felt for her zip and she stood firmly as he slipped his hand through the gap. She was bare and he immediately felt her fur and longed to know if it was the same colour as her hair. It was the middle of the afternoon, practically broad daylight too, for god's sake.

She was standing by the car when he got out and she smiled at him as if surprised that he'd followed her. He put his hand in his pocket and brought out her money.

'You dropped your cash,' he said, giving it to her. She took it but laughed. 'It doesn't matter. I ripped the bar take.' She pulled out a sheaf of punts from her pocket.

'The bar take?' he asked.

'Yes, I took the till, here—have half.' And she thrust about a dozen notes into his hand. He stood looking at her bewildered but she patted his cheek.

'Go on, put them in your pocket. We're going back to my place.'

She got in the car and he walked round and joined her. He glanced over at the taxi shed but there seemed no point going over now. His bag was gone. He was totally lost too, but they seemed to be moving into a better part of the city. He wondered if they were near the school he'd been at in the morning. The houses were bigger, the gardens well-kept with trim hedges just about eye height so you couldn't look in.

He began to think about what was going to happen when they got to wherever they were going. He was embarrassed by his bladder. All that water at lunch and that early tea break. There was nothing for it; he'd have to ask straight away. He thought she'd live in a flat but they stopped at a sizeable house and walked between the hedge to stand in a porch while she found keys. He laughed in what he hoped was a self-deprecatory manner.

'I'm desperate for a pee.' She held the door open for him. 'Straight up the stairs on the left.'

He found a biggish bathroom—shower, bath and bidet. It looked like there was money here. He peed, washed himself and stood in front of the mirror for a moment and practised a smile which he thought would be an appropriate way to look when he got downstairs. She was just shutting the front door when he got downstairs. Standing in the hall where she'd just placed it was his briefcase.

'My bag,' he said.

'Yes, I had it in the boot of the car. Can you manage a second tea?'

He followed her into the sitting room or rather he should say a drawing room. There was a coal fire brightly blazing. There were armchairs, a sofa covered in a flowered material with a creamy background—was that what you called chintzy? Sitting in one of the chairs before a small table with a tea tray on it was a well-preserved grey-haired lady. It was clearly her mother.

He was introduced as one of her colleagues.

'He's quite famous really, at least he's very well known.'

They seemed to have been expected because there were three cups on the tea tray and a little pile of crumpets on a brass stand in front of the fire. Her mother reminded him of his mother. She rattled on; how nice it was to meet her daughter's colleagues. Of course in her day one didn't really have colleagues because of course she hadn't really ever expected to work. She had the same Irish lilt in her voice but with an imperious quality to it. She was on now about the big house they'd owned in the west of the country; she described its location minutely, assuming he knew the area intimately whereas he'd never been outside Dublin before.

He commented on the crumpets, thinking they were an essentially English tea-time delicacy. That led her onto teas in the old days. There would be maids bringing in the scones and the cakes. Her daughter removed their more modest tray. She had hardly said a word since they'd come into the room.

There was an almost awkward silence after the tea things had gone, and then her mother remembered her well-bred manners and began to ask her guest a little about himself.

'Are you staying long in Dublin?' He looked at his watch.

'Actually, I have a ticket for the seven o'clock plane to London but I might . . .'

'You've plenty of time to catch it. You'll drive him to the airport won't you?' Her daughter nodded and they both got up and he made his thanks for the tea.

He picked up the bag and followed her out to the car. He put the bag where he always put it in front of the passenger seat and swung his long legs over it. He said what a charming old lady her mother was, and the girl suddenly revealed a similar capacity to chatter. She told how the old lady hardly went out now her husband was dead and how she worried about her being lonely. How nice it was for her to have visitors.

They got to the airport and she parked the car and came in with him. She stood by him while his ticket was checked and came with him to the ultimate gate through which the passenger alone passes. She turned towards him, took his head in her hands again and kissed him pushing her tongue between his lips. Then she spun him round and half pushed him through the barrier which lay beyond her. They had to walk across the tarmac to the plane. He walked quickly across to the plane, one hand swinging his briefcase, the other in his pocket handling a little bundle of Irish punts.

He was the first to mount the steps to the plane. He turned and paused at the top looking back at the airport buildings to see if she was still there. But it was getting dark and there were only dim shapes standing at the windows. It seemed foolish to wave at them. The next passenger on the step below was glaring up at him. He turned round and ducked into the plane. It had all the reality of a dream.

IN THE COMMONPLACE
ROOMS

I went into the secret rooms
considered shameful even to name.
But not shameful to me—because if they were,
what kind of poet, what kind of artist would I be?

—C. P. Cavafy*

I T WAS IN THE WINTER of '52/'53. I can't now be precise about before or after the new year but it was cold, that I do remember; bright, clear and frosty and I was returning to my rooms ... The smoke from my cigarette was enhanced by the mist my hot breath induced. It looked good. I practised my new skill of inhaling and puffed the air out before me, creating clouds that disappeared as rapidly as they appeared but for a moment created a halo around me. I was returning to my rooms ... I'll digress, my rooms ... No I won't ... let's get there first and onto the remarkable events of the evening.

I had been on Scotch Ale, topped up by a little rum. But was reasonably sober and was returning to the still monastic room in the fourteenth-century college and there dimly veiled in my room was a lady. My hand reached to the main light switch but before it was on, she had flashed out 'No more light' and obediently my hand froze and we were left with the lights reflected off my desk by the little table lamp which I had earlier left on. It provided barely enough light for us to inspect each other by. My guest was not, as I first thought, veiled, I realised, but over her tresses of . . . black hair I guessed . . . she had some soft material which came down either side of her face to give those soft and scarcely visible features a firm margin like the frame to a picture. Below I could dimly detect a slender body but it was covered with loose-fitting garments so that I was only able to guess at the slenderness, indeed the desirability, of the body of my guest.

I hesitated then on the threshold of the room wondering about some vague witticism like 'How nice of you to call', but settled eventually for the more solid 'Why have you come?' and to meet that reply that only occurs in fantasies. 'To satisfy your desires.' This was the veritable fantasy of which my nights were made. 'Aren't you,' she went on, 'going to offer me a drink?' Here was an immediate problem. I had none but quickly thought that in an emergency like this—there was good old Julian. 'I'll get some,' I cried, 'wait, wait,' and hastened out of the room back down the stairs and into the next staircase.

Julian was wealthy I had discovered early on in our acquaintance. Together with another friend, I had taken to dropping in on him soon after midday and sipping some of his madeira, indolently talking about—well what? We had few intellectual pretensions, I and my companions, although my neighbour was writing a novel, or more of an adventure story—a girl with raven hair and ice-blue eyes, an island, treasure, a young man and a yacht—yes, I swear it had all those ingredients in it.

This was back, you see, in that peculiar early post-war era, it was before, for example, the bomb. Not the explosion at Hiroshima, but before it had done anything to most people's consciences. We innocent youths just thought it had won us the war, we troubled no more about it. We drank South African sherry without a twinge as it slipped nobly down. We asked our servants to bring the shaving water later so that we could lie in on Saturday morning. We put on our suits on Sunday though and attended some religious ceremony. Afterwards we drank in a public house before our luncheon and passed the afternoon in some leisurely way, drank port after dinner every Sunday night. We were a gilded youth—I thought that often—'These are our salad days.'

That is not to say that we, I, had no pretensions to some sort of intellectualism. My new friends used to say to me, 'You, Chris, are an intellectual snob.' I agreed. From all I did and all I said let no one try to find out who I was. I knew about (hadn't read of course) Marx; could and had argued against the Irish Jeremy—a student who was a Marxist but not of the kind who rushed off to join the lines outside a factory, marched with banners in the street as they would today—no, he simply tried (and failed) to convince me of the solidarity of Marxism as an intellectual argument. Well my other friends cast Jeremy off (one of Chris's queer friends). For them he was socially outcast because he would not spend an afternoon looking over waistcoats at the tailor's. I was leaving him behind or aside intellectually, rejecting already anyone who claimed they could solve all the problems with one philosophy—including here my own personal difficulties, the difficulties of . . .

Well, those really relate to that lady. Here I was creeping into Julian's room; I knew he'd have madeira but at this late hour with a lady it seemed an improbable drink so I risked turning his light on and peered into the recess of the old black college sideboard and found a foil-capped bottle which looked like champagne—looked at the label—'Black Lansing'. I had never heard of that breed or many breeds, not sipped the stuff since on that day way back in '45 when my father had opened a bottle to celebrate a victory in some war or other. I picked it up reverently, grabbed two suitable looking glasses of Jules's and I marched to the lady in my room, pausing in the quadrangle to light another cigarette (it required me to put down both bottle and glasses on the turf) so that I could walk into my room, cigarette in my mouth, allowing smoke to drift back past my cheeks and say in a voice which I mistook for sophistication, 'Will Black Lansing do?'

My lady had kept on the desk light so I had been able to put the bottle down on the table, pull my cigarette—thumb, fore- and middle finger around it—out of my mouth to make this remark, but she merely nodded her head so I had no lead to direct any further remarks. As the university was in those days virtually celibate I could only guess that this woman was some ghost from the medieval past. There were those cloisters round which I liked to walk where I had been told a nun walked weeping and wringing her hands. (How does one wring one's hands, I used to wonder.)

Any rate there was evidence that in times past women had been allowed into this pasture to which now their—I was going to say, gentleness, but in these latter feminist days dare one use such a word?—was not allowed to wander. The fact was the nun walked alone and as she was weeping, presumably sadly. I also went round those cloisters alone—it was almost an embarrassment to admit a liking for that stone-roofed, flagged-floored walk with its grass, its tree. Therefore I walked, not thinking I was sad —because sadness (and presumably weeping and hand-

wringing) means missing something or more usually someone (for the nun it may have been her God) and that
missing requires previous knowledge of what you now lack
and I lacked that knowledge.

Of course if I'd known it, there was no lack of ladies if
one needed them in that college. There was a group (and I
crept along too) who went out hunting (well, beagling, a
poor man's sport as they said loudly) and the loudest of
them used to stand drinking from a flask with two or three
girls in silk headscarves behind a haystack at the hunting,
not in fact doing any real hunting. He had a key to a side
door and ladies came and went to the beds of him and his
colleagues by day and by night.

I myself didn't exactly lack ladies. Many girls, I was just
learning to my surprise, came if you called. Offer to go
dancing with them and they said yes, kiss them and they
kissed you back, begin to let your hands wander and probably they would be tolerated; although there were
inhibitions, prejudices still about that sort of thing but that
wasn't the quality of my loneliness. Mine was of my own,
not knowing who I was and therefore quite unable to offer
myself to anyone and not even knowing that these days and
nights I passed alone in '52/'53 were days I would never find
any more—they were mine entirely by chance, and so easily given up, then longed for painfully. How paralysed I was
—how cowardly, why did I keep my lips sealed while my
empty life wept inside me, my desires wore robes of
mourning.

Well now, coming to my lady then: 'Who was she?' As
champagne loosened my tongue and I began to talk I had
the immediate impression that I knew the lady or that her
conversation was or would be familiar to me. It was not

déjà vu or rather only the first half of the sensation; not—
I have been here before, but rather—I am going to be here
in the future. She was someone I knew well—or could
know well. So what did I talk to her about? Gossip. 'Do you
know anybody else in this college?' A slight shake of the
head and I began to fill her in. The man upstairs was rather
broad, I suppose you might almost say stout. He moved as
if there was something wrong with his neck, paused after
you had spoken, rocked his body slightly and then said,
'Interesting, interesting, most interesting. I'm most interested in your view of that subject, most interested.' One felt
like he was a gramophone who one wanted to kick on and
what my lady asked was, 'What will become of him?' It was
a question I'd never asked myself about any of us but I said
at once, 'A bishop.' 'Right,' she said, 'he will,' and she smiled
at me and I was tempted to throw myself on my knees and
pull her to me. To have been so close so many times to
those sensual eyes, those lips, to that body I dreamed of,
loved—so close so many times.

But my hand which had strayed forward towards her
drew back and I began to tell her of another near neighbour G.—a man whose voice lacked the deep sonorous
tone of the bishop—and retained something of its boy's
treble, indeed it sometimes cracked. He was a tall man, jet
black curly hair, broad shoulders but slender waist; one had
to say that he was attractive. He had told me how recently
he had been invited to that sober meal of tea by a Scot,
Maclachan or some name like that, who had interest in G.'s
violin playing, said he was thinking of forming a quartet.
So G. had gone along expecting to find two others there but
he had found the Scot alone wearing his kilt and with huge
bony hairy knees prominently exposed. An invitation had
been issued to G. to sit next to him on the sofa but G. had

hastily sat in a chair and the short hairy Scot had promptly pulled another chair very close to him and G. had moved round the small occasional table which held the tea things and tea had proceeded like a mad-hatter's party with the two of them constantly on the move. G. had fled the tea party finally but as he told me about it I realised that he had learnt something about his own nature and that he was accepting that realisation willingly, with excitement.

I saw too that he (had) ended up the sort of person likely to compromise you thoroughly if you were seen around with him too often. I felt I should have to see less of him and I told this to her and I tried to explain to the lady about my reputation and the need to associate with the right people and as I floundered to explain my behaviour my lady raised her eyebrows and insisted about G. But this wasn't the whole story—that wouldn't be fair; the memory of his beauty serves better. There is another angle, seen from that he appears attractive, appears a simple, genuine child of love, without hesitation putting the pure sensuality of his pure flesh above his honour and reputation. Above his reputation? But society, totally narrow-minded, has all its values wrong. So my lady asked, 'What will become of him, how will he end up in this society?' And I couldn't place him in a job but a moment's thought and I replied, 'Unhappy.'

At that moment the clock in our tower struck three and other clocks round the town echoed it of course: but always our clock seemed first, ringing out as it did from the Bell Tower built separately from the chapel and cloisters as if to give its sonorous messages, which were of course anthems to a god, a special emphasis with their own chamber to dignify their telling of the hour and their call to worship. And the bell summoned us forth for the lady wished to walk, a bright moon had arisen and we crossed the Victorian quadrangle, walked in deep shadows along the medieval wall, came up by the corner of the Carolian building and looked at the garden.

The garden was (still is) encircled on two sides by the ancient wall of the city: on the garden side one could still walk along a parapet and peer through enclosures not now at an enemy but at the Victorian enlargements of the college and, between buildings, the sprawling urbanity of the town beyond. But looking down clinging to the wall itself were saxifrage, aubretia and below magnificent borders where peony, chrysanthemum, delphinium, all the classic English flowers, raged in the summer: landscaped out in the eighteenth century. In the midst of this garden there was a mound on which trees and shrubs now looked wild as if genuinely strewn there by nature rather than carefully nurtured by man and beyond the mound the grass lawns led onto a huge copper beech. Just beyond the extension of its branches one or two white metal Victorian chairs stood on the grass as if they were waiting for someone to arrange a formal party.

This scene even with the frosty air was startlingly revealed by the bright moon and brought to mind a jingle from a musical—which I found myself reciting aloud to the lady. 'It's true I've been led an amazing dance, But why should I ever complain? If I could be given a second chance, I'd live it all over again. Look at the weather and look at me, We're both in a summery haze, We're young and we're green as the leaves on the trees, For these are our Salad Days. Summer and Sunshine and falling in love—All sadness was foolish and vain; It has melted away in the heat of the day, And my heart is so full there's no room there for pain . . . Summer and Sunshine and falling in love with a lover who made me his wife, From the heart I can say on this glorious day . . . I am having the time of my life.'

And having done that I immediately started to tell her about Peter who has seen the musical six times. I had commented, 'You must like it a lot,' and he had said, 'Well it's something to take a girl to.' I also remembered how he'd commented about G. saying that 'he doesn't pull his weight in the college', that he'd become 'completely degraded'. Without waiting for her to ask I knew what Peter would become, a surgeon. His father held that position at a famous London hospital and when I met him twenty years later he'd pretend not to recognise me because he'd know that I had also become degraded; not like G. who he would remember and would explain his downfall, 'His erotic tendencies, condemned and strictly forbidden (but innate for all that) were the cause of it.' He might add then, 'Poor chap' with the surgeon's sympathy for the cancer patient who he has cut about but failed to cure. But me, he wouldn't know quite what it was I had done wrong, he might make a vague comment. 'His clothes were a terrible mess.' Or perhaps thinking I hadn't pulled my weight in his world he might kindly comment, 'He was soon used up.'

A curious thought about that struck me and I began to speak about my tutor. The man in the college who was responsible for my studies practised many of the vices that Peter, who seemed to admire that tutor, objected to. His drinking was legendary and my servant used to wake me each morning with the number of whiskies which the eminent doctor had consumed the night before. 'Twenty-eight last night,' he'd say, 'sir.' And I might reply groaning, 'I know, I was with him, half of those were mine.' This eminent doctor as the drinking went on might tell you an anecdote of his own life: 'I knew a man who would pay you to defecate on a glass plate held above his face.' But such a tale would never be expanded beyond that short statement and he would turn to question you about, 'That girl I saw you with?' The exceptional thing about him was that in spite of all his debauchery, his vast sexual experience and the fact that usually his attitude matched his age, in spite of this there were moments — extremely rare, of course — when he gave the impression that his flesh was almost virginal.

I was telling my lady all this then: the anecdotes, the gossip which fed my fevered imagination, that made me look for some life of my own which was distinct from — and would go beyond — the established, inadequate norm. But what I could not do was to formulate any sentences or utterances which related to her. I wanted to go beyond with her the accepted modes of love. I knew there was something more, something deeper that required exploring, not only the sensual world of which I am speaking but the city of her mind so that it would be familiar when I walked down the old road, shops, pavement, stones, walls and balconies and windows — it would all be mine and she would intrude into me taking no notice of all the defences which my society and my childhood had given me though I had not wanted it and I would have to confess to her with no consideration, no pity, no shame, they've built walls around me, thick and high. And now I sit here feeling hopeless.

She had drawn me back now to my rooms and we sat there drinking the last of the champagne and when the expensive drinks were finished and it was close to four in the morning, happy, they gave themselves to love. At least that was how it should have been. My lady was clearly offering me not a relationship with a girl in a headscarf behind a haystack but something more intense, something which

I had glimpsed would provide us with an emotional life of which neither of us had dreamt. I never found them again —all lost so quickly. Now these years later I can only think of that lady: and if I can't speak about my love—if I don't talk about your hair, your lips, your eyes, still your face I keep within my heart, the sound of your voice that I keep within my mind, the days of December rising in my dreams, give shape and colour to my words, my sentences, whatever theme I touch, whatever thought I utter.

Now you are wondering how did it all end that December (?) night of '52/'53, when I failed to take her up, when I delayed the physical love-making because I knew it led on to a relationship I could not sustain. What happened then? What happened was that she had become someone else. I became aware that sitting in the shadows of my room all that time had been another person, a man who when she sighed and turned away from me, came up and proffered his hand which she took and they moved away together. And as she went she sighed but smiled at me leaving me to myself and I saw them together then, her body was thin and angular, her pelvis rolled at him and I could see in his eyes a surprise as he realised at last that he had a girl who saw love as a gift, something willingly offered to any who dared to enter in. And they passed from me and, as I staggered dazed by the window, I saw them in the clouds winging away from me and a light wind dispersed the dark shreds of night and dawn came up over the roofs and leads of the medieval chapel.

You see what I was being offered here was a choice about what sort of life I should live, what sort of place I should like to inhabit, what sort of city I would dwell in. I could see, indulge like Peter in things the girls in their headscarves liked and this could lead to a good life, a house no doubt with family, but would it lead to the sort of life I really craved: if I drew back what kind of poet, what kind of artist would I be? No, I had to learn to travel into the secret rooms considered shameful even to name. That would be more in keeping, much more in keeping . . . than for me to find pleasure in the commonplace rooms.

* The Cavafy material in this story is drawn from the C. P. Cavafy *Collected Poems*, trans. Edmund Kerley and Philip Sherrard, Hogarth Press, 1975

THE BELLS ARE RINGING

MY GOOD FRIEND JIM, when asked to travel for this or that reason—lecture, talk, conduct business, whatever—has stopped asking for money in recompense: he just asks for hotel room, a blonde and a bottle of whisky. This direct approach has certainly cut down his travelling and he claims to have shocked a number of university registrars, company secretaries and the like and maybe he has. But I, travelling all the time will tell him the real reason they don't meet his demands in these distant places is not because they are shocked but because there are no blondes. Year after year I board these big jets, alight at unlikely airports, visit uncouth cities, stay in half-built hotels, always ready, willing for any experience that fate will offer me, but again and again there are no blondes.

Imagine therefore some pale faceless Southern American city and a vast hotel—static rumbling from cheap carpets to the palms of the ape-like floor managers—and porters who, sweating in the over-dried air, conduct one to one's plastic cuboid cell and leave one to exchange one crumpled shirt for another. Imagine therefore me heading down to the opening reception and there at the elevator a pale clear face, light blue eyes, long hair and a soft voice which answers my interrogation. 'Yes, I am going to the reception,' and there we are walking into a hyper-ballroom shaking hands with a line of officials and passing on beyond to the whisky. Me and a blonde.

Pushing on further into the room past the pay-bar collecting our drinks, we finally locate Peter. I introduce Sheila to him. 'You've met Christopher, have you? He's a bit of a rascal, but we like him.' He tapped his pipe and smiled at me. His greying hair, more than the years he has over me, have led to this paternal act which he'll put on once too often for me. But on this occasion it was OK because Sheila saw through him at once. When he pushed off to fill our glasses she looked up at me with a shy smile and said, 'Bit of a rascal, eh?' and I launched into a too-long account of Peter's character.

Soon we were summoned into the adjoining ballroom for the meal but thankfully we did not have set places so at least we could sit with whom we liked. Old American friends kept calling me over but I nodded, saying 'See ya later' and pushed onto an empty table. Only the crewcut Sean was persistent and joined us whereas the other five we sat with were all strangers to me. We were not encouraged to get acquainted because we had barely finished our tinned fruit cocktail before we found ourselves being addressed over loud speakers and the first speech of the evening was on.

Sometime later we got to the main speaker and it is a good thing we'd eaten because he proposed to entertain us with his own holiday slides. Now, admittedly these were somewhat special because he comes from the space agency and what he has are shot after shot from orbiting spacecraft of mother earth. The trouble with the earth, though, is that from that far up and with that much cloud cover the Nile really looks much like the Mississippi (only the other way up of course). Our guest of honour has done only one of his five or six carousels which I can see piled up beside him when I begin to be restless. Sheila is ready to go too and smiles sweetly at Sean and all three of us crawl in the half darkness out of the ballroom.

Conspirators outside in the dazzling foyer, none of us are quite sure what to do. My initial attraction to the girl remains but other feelings begin to assert themselves. Will she remain cool and relaxed as the relationship develops? She hasn't spoken much yet and maybe she'll turn out to be dumb with that awful American dumbness. So I hesitate, standing a little to the side while Sean who is talking hard, goes on talking. He's not been being slow I suddenly realise, when Sheila asks, 'What about you, Christopher?'

'Yes, I'd love to go to a nightclub—Where is there?' I ask the driver. 'Where can we dance and drink?' He looks us up and down. 'The nearest one is Sacred Hell,' he says, 'but I don't know if you'd like that.' 'We'll give it a try,' I say and we all bundle into the taxi, the girl in the middle, and we whirl down the ten blocks to Sacred Hell. Sacred Hell is a converted church. Coloured lights reverberate around the high altar. The side aisles have been raked into broad steps with satin cushions laid on them. The whole seems an invitation to an orgy and there's raucous rock music to encourage one on but there's also an element that holds one back from total abandonment; perhaps it's the classic fishnet tights and short skirts of the waitresses who clamber round and take our orders for whisky or perhaps it is us. Sheila, I can't say, but Sean is in his usual suit which is always absolutely conventional and looks always newly pressed. I guess he has two or three suits with him. Also perhaps this failure has something to do with the conversation he immediately starts with me across the girl. It's always the same with Sean: a bantering, capping each other type talk. He starts in on my suits always being crumpled. 'More style than yours,' I riposte feebly. 'Carnaby Street, I suppose, you Londoners,' and uneasily I turn my head away to drink the whisky because actually my suit is a Carnaby suit. It's worn as a compromise. I have to go suited in this world I work in and try to make the suit at least a little unconventional. But then here in Sacred Hell! Here I see are the young local people, mostly with open-necked shirts. They are a moneyed crowd. We paid well to get in but what we're in is the unconventional end of a provincial American City. The walls have notices for poetry readings and it comes to me that for years I've corresponded with a girl in this city, a writer who sends me for some reason, information about the Kennedy assassination: she has a direct line to Garrison, the New Orleans DA who thinks it was a CIA plot and duplicated sheets arrive every six months with more details, more weird insights into the vagaries of the report of the Warren Commission (a document I have not read).

While I've been thinking this, Sean has been rapping away to Sheila; his manner is pitched even higher than usual and I can see that, as with everything he does, he is competing hard—on this occasion with me. Maybe he does really want the girl but I suspect that his efforts with her are aimed at putting me down as much as any genuine desire for Sheila. An obvious move now would be to ask her to dance and I suddenly realise Sean's difficulty. This type of scene is strange to him and he does not really know how to dance here. So Sheila and I dance. And it is good. Matching my rhythms at once, smiling quietly at me, not hurrying me to talk and relaxing me so that when we sit down again I can let Sean blast away and only occasionally cut back at him. In the end he is forced into more serious conversation and as it's a year since we've seen each other we have things to discuss.

When it's time to go I would be happy to walk, but Sean can't imagine this. It's ten blocks and he bustles off to the phone to call a cab. Then he hasn't the necessary dime so Sheila and I help him out. I am holding her hand and as he hastens away with all our dimes she suddenly gives me one of those smiles I am beginning to long for and leans hard right against me. 'Poor old Sean,' she says. She's understood him all right I think—and me too? I lean back and put my arms round her. She accepts me and kisses me happily. I feel very relaxed.

Back at the hotel she is very assured. Outside her room I stand and hope to be admitted. 'No, not tonight but maybe tomorrow,' she says. 'Will you have dinner with me tomorrow night?' 'Of course,' she replies. Her refusal to go further tonight is firm. 'I want to wait until tomorrow,' she says. When I get to my room I find that I am still carrying her cigarettes so immediately call her up. 'Shall I bring them along?' 'No, I can manage without cigarettes till the morning.'

There are very obvious dining places near our hotel so in the end I ask one of the assistant managers who sits at a desk in the lobby if he can recommend a nice quiet restaurant where . . . I leave it unfinished but he's ready with a name at once and indeed recommends the restaurant very firmly. I'm too naive to see through this one and we bundle into a taxi and head off for this great little intimate place. It's a disaster because he's been recommending it to everyone and, as I breeze confidently in, it's like entering the ballroom last night. 'Come and join us,' a quick recognisance with the head waiter and there isn't a table for two —half an hour, sir—so there's nothing for it. 'We can fit two in—two small ones.' Sly laughs from the men looking at Sheila and glances from the two wives present but Sheila's greeting is conventional, polite, correct.

The men are going to needle me—I know that at once

but how are they going to do it? 'Of course, you English,' starts a professor of psychology. What's it going to be I wonder? The health service—I hope not—our trade unions—well that will just be boring—'You don't do much shooting, do you?' 'Shooting? Oh, you mean guns, no we don't go in for guns as much as you do.' And then most unwisely —'it keeps the murders down.' Everybody in America knows the high murder rate has nothing to do with guns and my protestation that it has is politely put aside.

'What do you want with them anyway?' I ask back. 'How many guns do you have in your house?'

'We have quite a bunch I guess but then I've got two sons. They like to kill small birds.'

'Sporting rifles,' I say, 'but do you have anything else?'

'Oh sure, I have a gun for self defence—keep it loaded with dum-dum bullets.'

'Oh sure, that way they remember it more.'

'Who?'

'Intruders.'

'You mean you'd shoot a burglar?'

'Oh sure.'

'But you might kill him.'

'I wouldn't kill him. I've been trained to shoot to maim.'

They've put me down all right; at one glance they knew I did not know how to shoot to maim. There's a good general laugh, not at the remark, but at me.

I dissect my lobster and then, like a good American put down my knife and eat with fork alone. As I drop my left hand to my side it's taken and squeezed, a strong grasp and a quick glance reassured me that if this has been an attack on my masculinity I have somehow emerged not only unscathed but actually stronger. I decide I'll attack back: 'What do you think you will do about a health service?'

There is no problem at the end of this evening. We go straight to her room and become lovers. So for the remainder of the meeting I make appearances for appearances' sake but all the time longing to disappear back to her room. No need to bore you with the details but it is just right. 'You've got to get the pace right, the rhythm,' she says. By that she simply means how much and how often and how long you're going to make love. She matches me; in fact I have a moment of uncertainty when I realise that she can more than match my pace and that sexually there is no question of me leading her. There are times when I say 'Shall we go out?' and she says 'No, no, not yet,' and I yield to her wishes.

So we have four or five days together. We attend the meetings and we sit where we can see each other but not where we can be seen together. I attend a few of the cocktail parties ducking in early, talking loudly and then going back to where Sheila is waiting in her room. My room I just visit to answer the calls from the message desk and wonder who calls me for breakfast and guesses where I am.

It is just an affair with a blonde, then. We each call and manage an extra day together in a hotel empty, in a town we can walk round together, looking at each other by this time sadly. Making promises that we both intend to keep about next year—it is not until nearly the end that I say to her:

'What did you think about the conversation we had about the guns?' And in that lovely quiet voice—I call it cool in my mind—but how can a voice be cool? 'You were right, Christopher. I had a cousin. I really liked him. He was a beautiful boy. They gunned him down.'

'What—what—where? How?'

At my home in . . . and she names a city—a big city right

in the middle of America—Midwest do they call it? And she tells me of some slight scuffle on a path with some man who was being rude to his girl and then the police shooting. All I can think of to say is, 'You live there?' and Sheila says surprised, 'Yes, that's my home.'

Afterwards, months afterwards, I wake at night in another continent thinking about that girl in the middle of that vast continent and I think of her with love of course but also I think of her with fear. Fear for her alone in that place where people are not nice. I think of her alone, the only blonde (I know there are no other blondes), the only blonde where men from some antique and archaic past argue about their drinks, their girls, their jobs, their houses, their politicians, their rulers, when the millennium will come, in a way that is not my way and never can be my way. Although they are connected with my civilisation I think they are connected with the end of it.

The last morning it is nearly midday when we leave our room. We are not exhausted with loving but we are becoming too sad to make love any more. We wander down town and look at the art gallery. Some millionaire has given the city his share of French Impressionist painters. They are good to look at. But there is something sad in them too, coming again from elsewhere with the bustle of life in a colourful alive city whereas the city we are in is fading away from me, only the girl beside me will remain in my mind, a lone figure in a lost land.

We walk in the hot afternoon back to the hotel to pack and to leave. At the airport we shall both weep. I will drink a lot of vodka in my plane and emerge my cheerful, jolly charming self in New York. But meanwhile the slow walk back to the hotel. Deliberately slow, a slow march. We are not dawdling or tired; indeed I can almost feel the bounce, the drive available in the body beside me. We could if we want dance and pirouette down the avenue but we are doing the Slow March together.

We are walking beside a long high wall which we cannot look over. The avenue is tree-lined. There are enough leaves on the ground for a gentle scuff of sound to come up with each pace we make. We are silent. And in the silence not a single bell begins to ring but three or four ring out — not in time — and indeed they ring discordantly. In the wall we come to a gate, a big wrought-iron gate. We look across a vast cemetery by no means full yet. We look across at the groups of chapels in the middle. One no doubt for each of the many denominations of religion that America is heir to. We look across and see not one but two, three, four funeral cortèges drawing up at their different destinations. Suddenly we too know why the bells are ringing. The Bells are Ringing for Me and My Girl.

WHEN CHILDHOOD ENDS

(For my very good friend Henri Sliwoski)

PIERRE WAS VISITING HIS best friend Raymond. They were planning their next joint campaign when Raymond was to visit Pierre's house and in his big playroom on the top floor they would advance their armies and successfully tackle the enemies who faced them. Suddenly Raymond's mother appeared although Pierre had only been there a short while. 'Your mother has rung, you must run quickly home, she wants you.' Pierre was allowed to go to Raymond's house on his own because they lived on the same side of the street so he could visit Raymond without having to cross any roads. He just had to put his head down and run and that is just what he did. Not looking back he ran straight into a man.

'*Achtung*,' said a voice and a lot more in a language that Pierre did not understand. The man that Pierre had run into was a big man wearing a big grey overcoat who had what looked suspiciously like a gun slung over his shoulder and he picked Pierre up and looked at him, pinching his cheek quite hard. Pierre stared back at him saying nothing: the man put him down saying something in a strange language and struck him firmly on the bottom. Pierre realised he was free to run on and run he did, his head held high looking for other walkers on their quiet residential street.

Pierre ran up the drive, rang the front door bell and pressed himself against the door so that when it opened he half fell into the house. 'What are you doing?' said his mother. 'A man,' Pierre began, but his mother was too anxious, too frightened herself to listen to the story of what had frightened him. She picked him up and kissed him. 'You will not be able to play with Raymond any more. The Germans have entered Brussels.' Pierre knew that the Germans had something to do with why his mother didn't like him playing soldiers but she looked at him and he thought, she's sad—would she cry ever? And he said, 'Can I go up and play with my soldiers?' and she said, 'You can go and play with your soldiers.'

His father's job was a problem. It wasn't something you could tell at school like Raymond's father who was a doctor. Pierre's father worked in an office but it curiously was at Raymond's that he learnt more when Raymond's mother introduced him to a friend of hers saying 'His father's big in import/export and does a lot of business with England.' From England came his father's friend Stephen. His father and Stephen were busy in the office for one or two days and Stephen would stay with them and he always brought presents for Pierre and his older sister Carol. Dolls for Carol and when he was little soft animals, bears, a rabbit, a lion cub, but then just before his sixth birthday the best present ever, a big box with twelve lead soldiers in it. Guardsmen with red jackets holding their guns with their silver bayonets fixed in front advancing towards the enemy.

As soon as Stephen was gone, leaving to catch a night boat back to England, Mother sent Pierre quickly to bed. She kissed him quickly, no story and said, 'Go to sleep.' She hurried downstairs. Pierre crept out onto the landing so he could hear the row. Actually, he could only hear his mother's voice as she half shouted while his father murmured back.

'I don't want him to have soldiers to play with.'

'It's like giving him those toy guns. He'll grow up liking them, he'll grow up wanting a gun himself. He'll want to fight.'

'No toy soldiers. You could see he loved them. He'll grow up wanting to be a soldier.'

'He will, he will. He'll want to be a soldier. He'll want to be in wars. He'll be killed. You'll see and it will be your fault.'

'Having soldiers must tell him most adults approve of war. Look how well they are made. They'll seem his most important toys.'

And again and again, 'He'll want to fight.'

He only heard one sentence from his father, his voice raised in frustration. 'I'm importing them, for God's sake.'

He got cold on the landing and long before the argument stopped Pierre crept back to bed. But when later in the year all the family were there at one of those family lunches with his grandfather who wore a furry old hat all the time, his grandfather said to Pierre, 'What do you want for Christmas?' and there was only one answer, 'Soldiers.' And his grandfather laughed and said, 'That will be easy for everyone and make us all some money.' Pierre looked at his mother but her eyes were fixed on her plate not looking up or joining in the laughter. Her husband was silent too.

Sometimes his father would take him down to his office, a bunch of rooms in one corner of a warehouse, piled high with all sorts of goods his father was selling. But after lunch his father took him into the warehouse and showed him a huge pile of crates, 'Britain's,' and he tapped them: 'Soldiers.' 'You will see they'll be in all the toy shops next week.' And they were. He saw them when he went shopping, his mother dragging him away from the toy shop windows saying, 'Why couldn't he have gone on just importing clothes?'

So very soon Pierre had an army. Only his sister (and he loved her for it) had been to a shop and bought four Belgian paratroopers, blue and red with baggy trousers but all the brightest troops given by cousins and uncles were boxes they got at a discount from his father's warehouse. They were English soldiers mainly but there were the three Scottish regiments. The Tartan Trousers, the Greys and the Scots Guards who were splendidly gilded with very firmly attached but mobile arms, their rifles shouldered; they had very firm stands and did not fall over easily. Then the main English Regiment with their hats like the policemen in Brussels so they were 'Policeman Hats', then the English Guard one foot behind the other and their bayoneted guns not shouldered but held pointing forward. Then there were others, the Khakis, the Cavalry, the sailors, the odd Red Indian, the Band. Mostly the tunics were bright red polished, unchipped below the fresh pink faces with their mouse-like features.

Mostly, of course, the soldiers fought in the playroom, the big loft-like room on the second floor of the house, but that last summer he and Raymond had brought them down into the garden. To understand that you have to have seen the garden. The house was on a low hill with a verandah at the back with ten-foot vertical walls at one side of which there was a steep flight of steps. Pierre could remember when he needed a helping hand to go down them onto the path which ran along the top of the garden, down to the centre past three terraced beds to the circular crazy paving area, beside which were the rose beds. At a certain time of the year hundreds of little purple flowers nestled in these upper steps and Pierre liked them because their smell reminded him of his tall, dark, beautiful mother. Beyond the rose beds was a low wall and over the wall was the tumbling wild rockery through which a stepped path weaved its way to the tennis court. One hot day last summer he and Raymond had fought—they always fought pretend enemies—and had fought him to the right, Raymond to the left, all the way down to the tennis lawn.

This summer they planned to do it again but for today, sent upstairs, Pierre simply set out the men for an advance across the playroom floor to the door. Scots on the right, the guard pushing forward in the centre and to the left the Cavalry who were always such a pain to stand up. He had not got them all in place when he heard the front door slam and his father shout for his mother and he shot downstairs catching his mother as she came out of the bedroom. His father was standing in the hallway still not moving on into the sitting room.

'The Germans have entered Brussels.'

'I know, I saw them on the street already.'

'Tomorrow the children must go to their cousins.'

The next day his mother drove them down to 'the cousins'. The cousins were all right. There was some joke about them not being real cousins which Pierre didn't understand then. At first it was holidays and that was all right—they could get out of the small town and get into the woods. The cousins' children knew where you could swim in the river and knew lots of children from the town: it all seemed friendly and easy when they had to go to the local school, until a big lad about twelve pushed through the group. Pierre was kicking a football and he took hold of Pierre pushing him against a wall and said: 'You're a Jew-boy, a Jew-boy, a Jew-boy,' laughed and then ran off.

And a few days later there was a noise in the night and when they came down in the morning someone had daubed whitewash stars on the windows and written on the doors 'There are Jews in this house.' The cousins were frightened. 'It is not safe for you. It is not safe for us. You must go back to Brussels.' There were hasty phone calls and they were put on a train back to Brussels and told their mother would meet them.

Which she did. But not looking herself—her hair usually so neatly groomed was hardly brushed. She was wearing one of her elegant dark coats but pinned to it was the star from the windows, the Star of David. She took their hands and said, 'Come, we must get quickly off the streets, we are living over the warehouse.'

Out of the station into the street, Pierre was half running as his mother dragged him and his sister after her. But then coming towards them were two men in those big grey over-coats. Was one of them the man who Pierre had run into? They stood on the pavement and they had to stop and one of them said in a thick foreign accent, 'Not so fast, Jew-girl, not so fast.' And he took his mother's jaw between his big thumb and forefinger and lifted it towards him and kissed her very firmly on the lips and then let go of her laughing loudly and, pushing past them he went on up the street.

Their mother grasped their hands and ran and this time he did run and this time she was crying as they sped on towards the temporary sanctuary of the small flat above the now empty warehouse.

'Why are we here?' asked Pierre. 'Why are we not in our own house?'

'It's been requisitioned,' said his mother.

'But what about our things, our books, our toys, my soldiers?'

'They are still in the house as we left them,' said his father in a vague effort to reassure them that life would yet return to normal.

'A Christian organisation will look after you. You are going a long way into the country. You will not see us again until after this war is over.'

So the very next day a stranger they didn't know came and took them back to the station, explained the changes in trains they had to make and wrote down the name of a small town which they had never heard of down near the frontier with France.

Towards evening they arrived and were met by a tall bald man called Rupert and his wife Olga. They went quickly out of the station where Rupert had a small trap waiting and the horse briskly trotted of out of the town away, away to the small village where the pair lived.

They took them into the house and sat them down at a table with a meal they must have left prepared and they ate in silence. Then Rupert led them into the sitting room and sat them down on two hard chairs—Pierre's feet did not reach the ground. He sat opposite them and Olga sat beside them.

'You children must forget that you are Jews. You must forget your visits to synagogues—your Jewish prayers.' (Pierre heard his father's light laughing voice: 'We're not part of that synagogue crowd.') You must put all that behind you. Here you must be and be seen to be Christians. And that is good for you because Christ is the true faith, his is the true Church and you are going to become part of it. So you must learn to pray. We will start now. We will all kneel and you will repeat the prayers after me.' They all knelt and Rupert, line by line, pausing for them to repeat after him, began to intone:

'Our father who art in heaven
Hallowed be they name
Thy Kingdom come
Thy will be done . . .'

Afterwards Olga showed them the outdoor toilet and then took them up to their separate bedrooms. Olga left Carol in one little room and took Pierre into another room. He looked round and asked 'Is this a child's bedroom?'

Olga replied, 'It is your bedroom, Pierre.' But if it was his room why were there no books, like his old picture books and the newer books with stories he could read, and the books his mother read to him before his light was put out, although the door was always left open so that the light from the landing came in? Where were his toy animals, his cars, his rubber mini-bricks? It was true there was one book, a big heavy bible with a prayer stool before it. There was a bowl to wash in and a small chest for his few clothes. He had in his little case Benjamin—the rabbit—and he was allowed to take him to bed with him.

'Are you all right, Pierre?' Olga asked.

'I'm al right,' said Pierre.

'Good night then,' she said and put out the light and left the room, closing the door firmly behind her.

In the morning there were prayers before breakfast, a simple meal, then a journey in the trap to the village school where Rupert dropped them off and went on to the big sawmill where he was manager. The first morning he got down from the trap and led them through the gate and showed them the two doorways 'Boys' and 'Girls'. 'You go in there,' he said pointing. Pierre, scared that his companions might repeat the Jew-boy episode, found them instead cowed but friendly. Infringements of any sort were dealt with summarily with strokes of the cane on the hand while for what were regarded as more serious crimes — rowdy behaviour — you were caned smartly on the behind. You tried not to step out of line. So you worked in school and you had mounds of homework, much of it tedious in the extreme, pages of long division sums, long texts to copy from religious manuals like the sermons of Bernard of Clairvaux.

In the holidays, Pierre usually went to the saw-mill where he was busily employed stacking logs, clearing the floors of dust and digging in the surrounding vegetable garden. It was less boring than being at 'home' where you sat and read on through the great bible. There were the ritual prayers that had to be learnt but also there were extempore prayers and half sermons. On Sunday when they went to the chapel there were longer sermons. Pierre learnt that everybody was a sinner, the world was like it was today because of his sin. Rupert extemporised prayers every evening. 'For we know we have sinned and we suffer for it. Forgive us our transgression, heal us with thy mercies.' His sister soon seemed to catch the faith. She began to bend forward with clasped hands and occasionally even moaned a little as she bowed her head. But Pierre knelt uncomprehending and unmoved but anxious to know what had been his sins: his mother had not wanted him to play soldiers.

'Children are lucky. They have no work. They only have to find out about life when they have to work,' Olga stated regularly. Pierre felt he knew already what work was like, it was a daily grind, an unrewarding drudge.

Actually Pierre was lucky. He learnt Latin quickly and

was given books to study that other pupils couldn't tackle. There was a little library of texts which clearly his teacher had never read, Catullus, Ovid, which were a little different to the dry Aeneid and Caesar. It seemed he was 'clever', top of the class but he kept quiet about it, so it didn't bother the other kids who he regularly helped with their work.

This was the life then *pendant la guerre*. You grew, you learnt, your body changed (which you were well aware of and you could sin then but you would not talk of that), you inhabited a house, you lived in a village, you went to a school, you had no word from the past. The war ended but there was no word from your parents who had not even known the address you were going to, only the station where you were to alight.

His sister, in the summer of '46, went to Brussels. A letter came, she had found their mother living in a little room in the apartment of one of their old maids and then came his mother, a tiny little bent white-haired figure who clasped him in her arms and wept. Their father was dead in some camp (Auschwitz?). She stayed only the day and went back to her little room and soon his sister went after her to live and look after her.

But Pierre stayed. Now going by bus to school in the small town and still living with Olga and Rupert and more years passing; scholarships and going with his scholarship, but in a special scheme, south to Lyon to study medicine while his sister tried to recoup the family fortune by work-ing as a clerk in an import/export office. There was a small flat where Pierre could visit and stay for a little time with his mother who talked little but liked to have him there.

Pierre was a quiet serious student and then a quiet seri-ous young doctor down there in the hot South of France, not very socially adept you might say but always polite and considerate.

Then a dark-haired girl, a nurse, said, 'You are too serious, Pierre.' And when he looked at her she took his hand and held it for long enough for him to know that he wanted to hold her which he did. Warmth. You talk about the present and what you do. But you also talk to each other about the past—hers a bustling Provencal family. His? She told him to go back and look for it again.

So that summer he went back, stayed with his little silent mother and one day he walked the three or four miles to the suburb where the house had been. He recognised the road and came to the first of the houses in that peculiar almost gothic-style, smaller than their house but suddenly the old feel of the street. It was some time before he could work out that this apartment block of sixteen flats was where their house had been. There was a parking lot where the drive had been. He went to the back. He worked his way round there to the narrow road from which you peered over up at their garden. The garden had gone of course, the rockery, terraced flower beds, bulldozed out roughly, leaving only brown grass which led out from the back of the apartments.

The house in which his elegant mother, his quiet firm-handed father had had their life had not just been sold off, it had been destroyed. He went back to the front of the new apartments and looked up to where on the top right the playroom had been. The room was deserted, dusty, decayed, but oddly still there. And he thought that in there, still quietly standing to arms, would be the soldiers standing ready to advance. On the left he imagined the Cavalry might indeed by now be quite clouded with cobwebs and the poor animals would hardly be able to move at all. On the right the creaky board on which the Scots had stood so firmly had slipped and the three regiments had tumbled all together to the ground. But in the centre the guard, or at least some of them, would be still standing foot thrust forward to advance, their uniforms alas no longer bright red but chipped, faded with a leaden colour peering through. But others had fallen to the ground and were supporting themselves on elbows, their faces no longer fresh pink but greyish and their pin-point eyes no longer sparkling but glazed over as they still stared ahead at a doubtful future. This is, after all, what happens to old soldiers when childhood ends.

JUMP UP AND DOWN, YOUR MAJESTY

Celestine and Maximov
Are Going to Give
A Party
You Are Invited
To Jump Up and Down

(The Party takes place in any capital city which has parks, palaces, malls, walks, concert halls and people willing to partake of joyous pleasure. If you decide to give this party we suggest you hire a good lawyer in case you have trouble.)

ACT 1: A PUBLIC PARK

Through the trees (offstage left) four men appear, staggering with two huge poles made of the lightest possible material because they constitute the proscenium of a theatre. They hoist the poles erect, separate them by some twenty yards and hang on a cord between them a curtain. The stage is set. The guests assemble in front of the stage.

The curtains are pulled; on the grass behind them are twelve packing cases. From the extreme left packing case, a trumpet emerges playing a single note. The trumpet rises up and is followed out of its case by Henry. He tootles a note at the next case and a clarinet begins to ascend followed by Art. The third case is particularly large; it contains a double bass, while the fourth contains a guitar player and the fifth Trevor with his entire drum kit. They all play 'The Leopard and the Lady in Love' (music: Lowther—Words: Brock).

During this number, indeed chanting the words, Maximov and Celestine—the hosts—emerge from packing cases six and seven. The remaining five packing cases each contain a pair of dancers. Their names are (giving the ladies' first, of course), Alazais and Barthelmy, Algaia and Pathua, Gaillard and Berenger, Gauzia and Othon, Eslarmande and Fabrisse.

Maximov and Celestine cry, 'Welcome to our Party!'

The whole company jump up and down.

They begin to jump together. Music: 'The Joint is Jumping' (Waller). They circle the musicians, dancing at first together in pairs, and then the musicians themselves begin to move. The dancers split and dive into the audience finding new partners. The park and the guests are jumping. The proscenium collapses. The jumping guests are dispersed throughout the park.

ACT II: DOWN BY THE RIVER
The guests assemble on a grassy river bank in the centre of the city. A huge trireme is rowed slowly upstream towards them. It is rowed by chartered accountants, stockbrokers, company directors and ex prime ministers. The overseer is a huge African novelist. He won the Prix Concorde last year. He carries a crocodile hide whip. He uses it only on the fattest stockbrokers

On the top deck the party continues. Hosts and guests are dressed as Bachantes. Tables are laden with the remains of a banquet. They amuse themselves by squeezing grapes over each other and licking the stains from each other's flesh. They refresh themselves with rich red wine from the south. The wine is the blood of our lady (Cabestanh's lover). Strains of troubadour songs drift across the water to the company on the bank.

When the barque reaches the bank it sinks quite slowly, so those on the upper deck are at first unaware of their impending immersion. A few of the rowers are less lucky, they drown chained to their oars, but most are released in time. The party-goers dive into the water and swim to the side. They clamber up the bank and laughing and shouting rush through the crowds and are dispersed into the city.

ACT III: TEA AT THE PALACE

A hundred guests are invited to this Act. In the mall that leads to the Queen/President/King/Emperor's palace, fifty old brass beds are drawn up in ten rows of five beds abreast. Each bed has been equipped with an electric engine borrowed from the city's milk floats. They are stationary until it is time for tea. The guests, two to a bed, usually a man and a woman together, but like-sex couples are accommodated, are sleeping off their luncheon (which they had, you'll recall, on the trireme). The men are wearing striped flannel pyjamas and nightcaps. The ladies are wearing Victorian linen nightdresses.

Celestine with Maximov, of course, is in the central bed of the front row. She awakes, stretches, snatches a megaphone from under the sheets and cries out, 'It's tea time.'

Girls and men awake. The men start their engines, the girls

release from under the sheets white doves which have been nestling there. The cavalcade advances. They have streamers to toss at the crowds, party squeakers to blow, penny whistles, toy trumpets and crackers large enough to be pulled between the beds (which are steered, incidentally, rather like boats, with tiller lines which gently control the front wheels).

They arrive at the palace. In front of it there is a large and ornamental fountain. The beds swing into line abreast round it. The couples stand to attention—the men adroitly handling the tiller lines, the girls all now in paper hats from the crackers—and salute smartly. When the third row of beds is immediately opposite the palace gates, all raise their megaphones and bellow in unison through them: 'Jump up and down, Your Majesty!'

Fifty yards down the mall there is a convenient flight of steps. Here the couples dismount, form up into ranks and march up into the city singing:

The brave old Duke of York
He had ten thousand men,
He marched them up to the top of the hill
And he marched them down again.

They disperse into the city. Again? Well, yes there are a lot of slightly drunken people dispersed about the city.

ACT IV: CELESTINE AND MAXIMOV'S NUPTIALS
A huge circular hall. In the centre the band is esconced. They play merrily throughout the evening and on into the night. Around the walls are tables with drinks and food. It

is a good floor for dancing on. There are circular daises arranged in a circle around the hall. On each of these a bridegroom awaits his bride. Maximov and Celestine and the five dancing couples from the morning are six of the couples; the others are Mathena and Guillaume, Gentile and Jacques, Vuissane and Arnaud, Allemande and Pons, Alissende and Guilhabert, Mengarde and Prades.

The bridegrooms wear robes which might be (but are not) the habits of Franciscan monks. Behind them are high couches on which, in time, they will lie. Two acolytes serve them. In time they will disrobe them but now they kneel, holding up before the bridegrooms twelve texts which, as soon as the brides enter, the bridegrooms begin to intone. Each has a different text. They are as follows: Instructions for the design of a cyclotron; the details of the structure of a combine harvester; foot by foot cross-sectional blue-prints of a machine for making sandpaper; a descriptive account of the first water closet; instructions for sterilising contaminated water; the house surgeon's report on a total hip replacement; a description of the organ installed in the University Concert Hall in Mexico City; a Victorian recipe for chunky bitter marmalade; instructions for the computerisation of the traffic control system of the city; a handbook on five centuries of type faces; an interpretation of the golden section and the anatomy of the body beginning with the toe. It is this last text which Sir Maximov reads. This is Sir Maximov's text:

'Beneath the skin and nail fibrous tissue covers the bone of the terminal phalanges which proximally relate to the metatarsals. The metatarsals are surrounded by lumbricals and interossei muscles and along them stretch the long flexors and extensors of the toes within their tendon sheaths. The metatarsals relate proximally to the tarsal bones. There are five tarsal bones: they are the calcaneum, the tallus, the cuneiform, the cuboid and the navicula; they together constitute the ankle joint. The calcaneus forms the heel (the heel, thought Sir Maximov, this is a blood awful anatomy textbook). It is into the calcaneum that the tendo Achilles inserts. The tendo Achilles has two muscle bellies which contribute to its origin. They are the gastrocnemius and soleus muscles. The talus relates to the tibia and the fibula – the two bones which make up the lower leg. Other muscles surrounding the ankle joint include peroneas longus and brevis and tibialis anterior – the main ankle flexor. Medially the distal end of the tibia forms the medial malleolus whilst laterally the end of the fibula forms the lateral malleolus. The bones of the lower leg relate of course to the femur . . .'

The brides in all their glorious white regalia are led in by their four maids. Their veils are lowered and they parade to the strains of various familiar wedding marches for a complete circuit of the hall. They are conducted to their grooms. During the march the grooms have read in a low monotone, but now they raise their voices and give tongue a full octave higher than before. It is the moment of the disrobing of the brides. The bridegrooms are allowed one gesture — they themselves lift up their lovers' veils — but they do not falter in their reading while they do this. The maids disrobe the brides (for a fuller account of this see Marcel Duchamp).

It is the moment for the disrobing of the grooms. The maids assist the acolytes to lift the grooms onto their couches and together they aid the bride on to her groom. They are expected to continue their reading but at a certain specific point in time the voice breaks off into a moan. It is a moan of joie. It could not be said the party is over — the party has just begun.

Jump up and down your Majesty